HAPPY BIRTHDAY, LEXIE!

"Mom," Lexie said shakily, "just what are you suggesting? Do you want me to say I'll join up with Shirley and have one great big jolly party together with her or something?"

"I'm not making any suggestions, Lexie. I'm just hoping you and Shirley will be able to work something out together—something that will make both of you feel happy about your birthdays."

"Well, I don't care what Shirley wants!" Lexie screamed, bursting into tears. "I care about what I want! You promised me I could have a good party this year, for the first time ever! It was supposed to be the best party I've ever had—the perfect party I've been dreaming about my whole life long! But now you're trying to make me change all my plans—just to suit Shirley Spitzer. Well, I won't do it! If the only way I can have a party is to share it with someone as weird as Shirley Spitzer, then I won't have a party at all!"

Happy Birthday, Lexie!

LISA EISENBERG

PUFFIN BOOKS

PUFFIN BOOKS

Published by the Penguin Group

Penguin Books USA Inc., 375 Hudson Street, New York, New York 10014, U.S.A.

Penguin Books Ltd, 27 Wrights Lane, London W8 5TZ, England

Penguin Books Australia Ltd, Ringwood, Victoria, Australia

Penguin Books Canada Ltd, 10 Alcorn Avenue, Toronto, Ontario, Canada M4V 3B2

Penguin Books (N.Z.) Ltd, 182–190 Wairau Road, Auckland 10, New Zealand

Penguin Books Ltd, Registered Offices: Harmondsworth, Middlesex, England

First published in the United States of America by Viking Penguin,
a division of Penguin Books USA Inc., 1991
Published in Puffin Books, 1993

1   3   5   7   9   10   8   6   4   2

LIBRARY OF CONGRESS CATALOGING-IN-PUBLICATION DATA

Eisenberg, Lisa.
Happy birthday, Lexie! / Lisa Eisenberg.   p.   cm.
Summary: Although she had hoped to make her tenth birthday extra
special, Lexie reluctantly agrees to have a joint party with an
unpopular girl in her class—with surprising results.
ISBN 0-14-034568-X
[1. Birthdays—Fiction.   2. Family life—Fiction.   3. Parties—
Fiction.]   I. Title.
[PZ7.E3458Hap   1993]   [Fic]—dc20   92-21107

Printed in the United States of America
Set in Times Roman

To my family, past and present

ONE

Lexie Nielsen picked up her fork and prodded the lumpy yellow mound of food in the middle of her plate. "What is this stuff, anyway, Mom?" she asked. "It looks disgusting."

"It's sesame tabouli chicken salad, honey," her mother answered.

"Well, it looks disgusting."

"I heard you the first time, thank you." Mrs. Nielsen looked at her youngest daughter and sighed wearily. "I know you don't like the food from Exotic Appetizers,

Lexie," she continued, "but I was running late today, and that's the only takeout place on my way home from school."

"But, Mom, this stuff is all stringy and slimy-looking, like a bunch of rotten squashed slugs. It reminds me of a riddle I heard at school yesterday. It goes: Why did the squirrel cross the road? Because he wanted to show the whole world he had guts! And that's just what this stuff looks like. Smashed squirrel guts or maybe . . ."

"Lexie!" her father interrupted sharply. "You've made your position abundantly clear. There's no need to make the rest of us sick!"

"If you can't bear to eat the salad," her mother said, "you may go into the kitchen and fix yourself something else."

Lexie jumped up from the table so quickly she almost knocked over her chair. She dashed into the kitchen, where she grabbed the peanut butter from the cupboard, the bread from the bread drawer, and the jelly from the refrigerator. While she was slapping together a thick, oozing sandwich, she reminded herself to ask her mother about going shopping for her birthday party invitations tonight. The party was only two weeks away, and it was important to get the invitations into the mail as soon as she could.

When she came back into the dining room with her sandwich, her father glanced at her plate. "PB and J again, Lexerino? You really ought to give a different cuisine a chance. I, for one, find this sesame whatever-it-is salad to be very, very tasty."

"So do I," said Lexie's older sister Faith.

Lexie made a face at her. "Quit faking, Faith. Stop pretending to be so sophisticated. You know you hate this stuff just as much as I do."

"I do not!" Faith said indignantly.

"Oh, really? Then why'd you pick out all the slimy parts and push them under your lettuce leaf like that?"

"What are you, Lexie, a CIA food agent or something?"

"Girls, please!" Mrs. Nielsen covered her ears with her hands. "Can't we get through just one meal without all this bickering between the two of you?"

"Well, she started it," Faith said. "I was just sitting here, minding my own business, peacefully enjoying my dinner . . ."

"Pretending to enjoy it, you mean!" Lexie broke in.

"Enough!" said Mr. Nielsen. "If you kids can't stop arguing all the time, we'll institute a new rule at the dinner table. Absolute silence for all people under the age of fourteen!"

"That's okay with me," Faith said. "That means I'd get to start talking on my next birthday, but Lexie would have to wait another four years!"

"Four years and fourteen days," Lexie said. "Which

reminds me, Mom. Do you think we could go shopping for my birthday party invitations tonight? I have to get them into the mail before it's too late."

"Oh, I'm glad you brought that up, Lexie," her mother said. "I have to talk to you about that very subject. I ran into the mother of one of your friends from school in Exotic Appetizers tonight, and she happened to mention that . . ."

Mrs. Nielsen was interrupted by the ringing of the telephone. She pushed back her chair and hurried into the kitchen to answer it.

"If that's one of your friends on the phone, Faith or Lexie," Mr. Nielsen said, "I want you to instruct them not to call at dinnertime in the future. Our meal is disturbed like this almost every single night."

"It's definitely not for me," Faith said. "It's probably for Karen. I must have taken a thousand messages for her in the last two days." Karen was Faith and Lexie's seventeen-year-old sister. She was a high school senior, and she'd been away from home for two days, visiting prospective college campuses.

"It might be for Daniel," Lexie said. "Even though he practically lives at McDonald's now, his stupid friends keep calling him here all the time anyway."

Daniel was fifteen and the only boy in the Nielsen family. Last month, he'd started a part-time job at McDonald's, and several evenings a week he came home smelling of greasy hamburgers and stale french fries. Between his new job, activities with his friends, and baseball practice, it seemed as if Daniel was almost never in the house anymore.

Mr. Nielsen put down his fork and helped himself to a banana from the basket of fruit in the middle of the table. "Speaking of riddles," he began.

"Oh, *please,*" Faith broke in. "Can't we be spared for even one night?"

"No!" Lexie said gleefully. "Go on, Daddy. Speaking of riddles . . ."

"I was going to say before I was so rudely interrupted," Mr. Nielsen continued, "that this banana reminded me of a riddle. What kind of shoes can you make from banana peels?"

"Slippers," Lexie answered immediately. "Daddy, that's about the oldest riddle in the whole world."

"Well, I beg your pardon," her father said, biting into his banana. "I still think it's very ap*peel*ing."

Faith and Lexie were still groaning when Mrs. Nielsen came back into the dining room. "The call was for me," she said as she sat down and picked up her fork. "It was Dorothy Spearles from the Penelope Dove campaign."

Lexie and Faith looked at each other and snickered. "Mom, who in the world is Penelope Dove?" Faith asked. "And how can she stand to live with a name like that?"

Mrs. Nielsen smiled. "I'll admit it's a funny name,"

she said. "But Penelope is *not* a funny person. She's a very serious candidate for a place on the school board, and I've volunteered to help out with her campaign. I just said I'd go over to her house tonight to help stuff envelopes."

Mr. Nielsen cleared his throat and put down his fork. "Aren't you forgetting, Barbara, that I have an Audubon Society meeting tonight?"

Mrs. Nielsen stared at him. "Again, Frank? Didn't you already have an Audubon meeting this week?"

"That was the regular monthly meeting. The meeting tonight is the special bird photography session. You know I have a picture entered in the annual contest. I'm sure I mentioned it to you."

"Well, I'm equally sure you didn't!" Mrs. Nielsen said.

There was a moment of charged silence at the table. Finally, Lexie couldn't stand it anymore. "Say, Daddy," she said loudly. "Speaking of riddles, I heard a great one today. Why is six afraid of seven?"

Mr. Nielsen didn't even seem to hear her. "Whether or not I mentioned it to you is not the issue, Barbara," he said. "The issue is whether you thought of checking with me before making a commitment for tonight."

"Did you check with me before you made your commitment, Frank?" Mrs. Nielsen asked. "Because I don't see why . . ."

"Because seven *ate* nine!" Lexie interrupted. "Get it? 'Eight' and 'ate'?"

No one at the table said a word, and Lexie gave her sandwich a savage poke. She hated it when her mother and father got into this kind of argument, but whenever she complained about it, her mother told her it was just a "discussion" and said it was important for children to see parents openly working through their grievances with one another.

Lately though, there had been too many of these "discussions" to suit Lexie. Whenever a discussion started, she wanted to crawl under the table. For one thing, everybody got crabby during the discussions. And for another, the discussions never seemed to solve anything. The same old topic came up again and again—without fail the problem was always *time* and how there just wasn't enough of it to go around. Ever since Mrs. Nielsen had gone back to school for her masters in counseling last fall, *time* was all anybody in the Nielsen family seemed to care about.

As Mr. Nielsen started to say something else about his Audubon Society meeting, Faith interrupted him. "I really don't see what the problem is," she said. "You can both go ahead and go to your meetings. Lexie and I can stay home by ourselves."

"No!" Lexie cried in alarm. "No, we can't, Mom. Faith might try to kill me or something."

"I don't know about that," Mrs. Nielsen said doubtfully. "But the last time we tried leaving you two home alone at night, the experiment was definitely *not* a success. Remember? Lexie called me up at the League of Women Voters meeting and begged me to come home!"

"But that was almost a whole year ago, Mom," Faith explained. "We're a lot more mature now. At least I am."

Lexie snorted, but Mr. Nielsen rubbed his chin and nodded. "It sounds like a plausible solution to me," he said slowly. "After all, the girls aren't little children anymore. They should be able to stay home for at least a few hours without murdering each other. And we probably won't be staying out very late. What do you think, Barbara?"

"Well, I don't believe either one of us will be back much before ten-thirty," Mrs. Nielsen said. "But if the girls lock the doors, and we both leave the phone numbers where we can be reached, I suppose it would be all right to try it again."

"Well, I suppose it wouldn't!" Lexie shouted. "You don't know what Faith acts like when we're home alone. She treats me like I'm one of the little Larsen kids she baby-sits for. She acts just like a South American dictator!"

"I have to act like a dictator!" Faith shouted back. "Unless I scream at you, you never do one single thing you're supposed to! You don't do your homework, you don't brush your teeth, you don't go to bed . . ."

"That's because you try to make me go to bed at about 6:30, because you're so power-hungry, you—"

"Quiet!" Mr. Nielsen thumped his fist on the table so hard the water glasses shook. When everyone gaped at him, he swallowed hard and made a visible effort to calm himself down. He turned toward Lexie. "Lexie," he said more quietly. "Faith will be in charge tonight, and you'll be expected to follow the normal evening routine, just as if your mother and I were at home." He looked over at Faith. "You on the other hand, Faith, will be expected to be reasonable and tolerant and . . ."

"And not bossy!" Lexie broke in.

"And not bossy," Mr. Nielsen concluded. He looked down at Mrs. Nielsen's end of the table and smiled. "Have we resolved our conflict in a way that's sensitive to our mutual needs, Barb? Are we comfortable with this arrangement?"

"We're comfortable, Frank." Mrs. Nielsen smiled back at him. When she'd first started taking classes in counseling last fall, she'd developed an alarming tendency to talk like a psychology textbook. At first the rest of the family had tolerated her jargon in pained silence, but after a while everyone had started poking fun at her. Fortunately, even though Mrs. Nielsen was very serious about her classes, she was also good-natured about all the teasing. Nowadays, talking "psycho-babble language" was an inside Nielsen family joke.

Mrs. Nielsen glanced at her watch. "Oh, dear," she said. "Look at the time. All our beautiful conflict resolution will be in vain if Daddy and I miss our meetings. We both need to be out of here in a few minutes. Whose turn is it on the dishwasher schedule for tonight?"

"Karen's," Faith and Lexie said in unison.

"Oh, dear," their mother said again. Then she got to her feet. "Come on, everybody. If we all pitch in and help, we'll have these dishes cleaned up before we know it."

In an unusual act of cooperation, Lexie jumped to her feet, picked up her plate, and hurried to the kitchen. She'd just thought of a plan for making her evening with Faith the Dictator slightly more bearable than usual. But in order for the plan to work, her parents had to leave the house *soon*.

Two

Fifteen minutes later when Mr. and Mrs. Nielsen were gone, Lexie sat down at the desk in the living room and began listing the names of the kids she wanted to invite to her birthday party. She'd only had time to write down one name—her own—when Faith came in and ordered her upstairs to brush her teeth and get her pajamas on. Even though it was an entire hour before her usual bedtime, Lexie was still strangely cooperative.

"Okay," she said cheerfully, putting down her pen and paper. As she stood up and headed toward the stairs, she spoke over her shoulder. "Oh, by the way, I noticed in *TV Guide* there's a rerun of *Chiller Theater* on tonight."

Faith didn't say anything, but her thoughtful silence told Lexie that her sister had taken the bait. Although Faith tended to be fussy and highbrow about most things, she had a strange weakness for creepy old movies and scary TV shows. Because Mr. and Mrs. Nielsen didn't approve of that kind of entertainment, however, she was almost never allowed to watch any of the programs she liked.

Lexie had known Faith wouldn't be able to pass up this chance to watch *Chiller Theater*. And she also knew that if Faith broke the rule about scary TV, Lexie would get to break the rule, too. Even though she hadn't been able to shop for party invitations as she'd wanted, at least she'd be able to salvage something from the evening. She'd get to watch a forbidden program *and* stay up an entire hour later than usual.

"When does it start?"

"Oh, in a few minutes I guess," Lexie answered casually. "Just enough time for me to microwave a bag of popcorn."

"Okay, hurry up. But if Mom and Daddy come home while we're watching it, we have to change the channel and pretend we're watching PBS."

"Okay," Lexie agreed happily. She ran into the kitchen, grabbed up a bag of popcorn, hurled it into the microwave, and set the timer. Three minutes and forty seconds later, she was curled up on the old green armchair in the corner of the living room. Faith was stretched out on the brown corduroy couch. Both girls were munching popcorn and watching *Chiller Theater*'s vampire host, Vlad, introduce the show.

Because she was planning to continue working on her party plans during the commercials, Lexie had her pen and paper on her lap. But before long, she became so engrossed in the program, she temporarily forgot all about her birthday. This week's *Chiller Theater* episode was called "The House by the Sea." It started off showing a handsome young married couple moving their belongings into a dead sea captain's house on a cliff right next to the ocean.

"Why do they keep hugging and kissing and laughing all the time like that?" Lexie demanded to know after a few minutes.

"Because they just got married, of course," Faith said. "And they're happy about moving into their first house."

"But the house is so dark and creepy," Lexie said. "And the husband's hair is greasy and his lips are too fat. I don't see how the wife can stand to kiss him so much."

Faith snorted. "Shut up and keep your disgusting, immature observations to yourself," she ordered. "Some of us are trying to watch the show."

Lexie made a face and started to answer back, but the show caught her attention again. Her pen and paper slipped to the floor, but she didn't even notice. Strange things were happening in the old house by the sea. Winds howled in the chimney. Floorboards creaked in the dead of night. Then the portrait of the old sea captain in the parlor started oozing seawater!

Lexie gripped both arms of her chair so hard her knuckles turned white. "Faith," she whispered. "What's going on? Why is the husband's hair turning white? And what happened to his leg? How come he's limping like that? And where did he get that accent?"

"I'm not sure," Faith whispered back. "But I think he's been possessed by the soul of the evil old sea captain who used to own the house!"

"Uh-oh." Faith was right. Before long, the husband was completely transformed into the sinister old sea captain. Then he started giving his wife long, menacing stares while she was sleeping. Lexie couldn't take it anymore. She moved out of her chair and scuttled over to the couch. She plopped down right on top of Faith's feet, but her sister didn't even complain.

"Why doesn't the wife just get out of there?" Lexie asked after another terrifying minute. "Can't she tell he's going to murder her?"

"Maybe she doesn't believe it's true. He is her husband, after all. Maybe she hopes he'll snap out of it."

"Well, I know I'd get out of there if I were her," Lexie said in a quavering voice. "Before it's too late."

Seconds later, the wife realized her danger and did try to escape into the stormy night. But all at once the husband/sea captain appeared out of nowhere and blocked the door. In the next hair-raising scene, the poor, sobbing woman fled up the spiral staircase to the tower room. There she huddled in a corner, listening in horror to the ominous sound of her sea captain husband slowly dragging himself up the stairs as he came to get her. Step-*thud,* step-*thud,* step-*thud.*

Lexie moaned and covered her eyes. "Faith, I can't watch. Tell me what happens."

"He's limping the rest of the way up the stairs," Faith whispered. "Now he's yanking on the door, but it's locked. Oh, good, he's turning back. No, wait! He's got an ax! He's chopping down the door! The wife's screaming her brains out."

"I can hear her! What's he doing now?"

"He's . . . he's . . . chasing her around the room. He's reaching out to strangle her. No, wait! He knocked over a candle. He started a fire!"

Lexie sat up and uncovered her eyes. She was just in time to see the husband come to his senses and drag his hysterical wife out of the burning tower. As the old sea captain's house burned to the ground, the man's hair turned brown again and everything went back to normal. Violins played, and the young couple kissed and hugged as if nothing had ever happened.

But Lexie and Faith didn't recover so quickly. When Faith pushed the button on the remote control and turned off the TV, the living room went completely dark, and they both gasped in surprise. Without saying a word to each other, they raced toward the stairs, turning on all the lights as they went. When they got up to their room, they put on their pajamas as fast as they could. All at once, they were dying to be under their warm, safe covers.

When they were both ready for bed, Faith started out the bedroom door. Whenever Karen went away for even one night, Faith hauled her things out of the room she shared with Lexie and moved into Karen's room. Faith always said she couldn't wait to have a little neatness and privacy in her life. She was loudly counting the days until their oldest sister went away to college permanently, because after that she wouldn't have to live with Lexie anymore.

But tonight she wasn't in her usual hurry to be by herself. "You know," she said thoughtfully, as she stood by the door, "that mattress on Karen's bed is really lumpy. My back has been hurting me all day."

"Maybe you should sleep in your regular bed in here for a while, then," Lexie suggested eagerly. "Just until your back feels better." She'd been dreading the idea of being all by herself in the big, shadowy bedroom tonight, but she hadn't wanted to admit it to Faith. Karen's lumpy mattress was the perfect excuse for Faith to move back in with her.

"Okay," Faith said.

Leaving the hall light on and their door wide open, the two girls scurried across the bedroom floor and jumped into their beds. They both lay still for a while, rigid with fear under their blankets. After a few minutes, Faith broke the silence. "Lexie?" she whispered. "Are you still awake?"

"Yes," Lexie whispered back.

"Did you lock the front door downstairs before we came up?"

Lexie jerked upright in her bed. "Me? Why should I have locked it? You're the big responsible baby-sitter who's supposed to be in charge tonight, remember?"

"I know," Faith said miserably. "But I forgot to do it."

"Do you want to go down and do it now?"

"No. Do you?"

"No."

Neither girl said anything else. There was no need to explain. Each of them knew why the other one didn't want to lock the door. The idea of going downstairs alone in the big empty house seemed not only terrifying, but impossible.

"Maybe we could both go," Lexie began. "That way . . ."

"Shhh! Did you hear that noise?"

"No . . . wait! Yes! *Faith!* Somebody's walking around downstairs!" She listened for another few seconds. She could definitely hear the creak of floorboards coming from downstairs. "It must be Daddy," she said. "Or Mom."

"It can't be!" Faith said. "They said they wouldn't be back before ten-thirty, and it's only ten o'clock!"

Instantly Lexie was out of her bed, scampering across the room, and burrowing her way into Faith's bed. For another tense minute, they listened to the noises from below. Then Lexie moaned. "Faith. The sounds are getting louder. The . . . the *thing* is coming up the stairs!"

"Oh, my gosh. Listen, Lexie. It sounds . . . just like the old sea captain!"

Lexie strained to hear. Sure enough, an ominous step-*thud*, step-*thud* sounded on the stairs. Lexie clutched Faith's arm and squeezed as hard as she could.

Suddenly, an enormous dark shadow loomed in the doorway. Lexie and Faith closed their eyes and shrieked at the top of their lungs. Then a hand reached out and snapped on the bedroom light.

When the two girls finally opened their eyes, they

saw their brother, Daniel, standing in the doorway. He had an Ace bandage wrapped around one ankle, and he was blinking at them in confusion. Gradually, the air filled with the smell of greasy hamburgers and stale french fries. It was the most beautiful aroma Faith and Lexie had ever smelled in their lives.

THREE

The next morning in school, Lexie was so tired she could hardly hold her head up. Even after her parents had come home the night before, and order had been restored to the house, she'd still been too terrified to sleep. Hour after hour, she'd lain wide awake in her bed, imagining she heard the step-*thud,* step-*thud* of the old sea captain, coming up the stairs to get her. It would be a long time before she'd watch *Chiller Theater* again, she promised herself.

"On yesterday's homework papers," her teacher, Mr.

Snyder, was saying, "I noticed that a lot of you are still making the same careless mistakes on the Cumulative Review pages."

Lexie yawned so hard her eyes filled with hot, itchy tears. When she glanced up at the big wall clock, she saw the numbers through a wavering, shimmering haze. She rubbed her eyes and looked again. Ten-sixteen! Only three minutes had passed since the last time she'd looked.

"For instance," Mr. Snyder droned on, "on the first problem where you were asked to identify a rectangular prism, almost half of you said it was a plain old rectangle! And on the problem about congruent figures, even more of you slipped up, even though we've been over and over this material again and again."

Again and again and *again!* Lexie thought. And it never got any less boring. She stifled another yawn. Since she hadn't even turned in yesterday's homework paper yet, she knew nothing Mr. Snyder was saying could possibly apply to her. She didn't feel the slightest bit guilty about tuning out his voice and concentrating instead on her latest daydream about becoming the world's youngest internationally famous prize-winning jockey. But in no time at all, an even more interesting topic came into her mind.

As Lexie turned her paper sideways and drew an elaborate picture of a birthday cake in the left-hand margin, the mental image of herself graciously accepting a wreath of roses in the winner's circle at the Kentucky Derby quickly faded. *Party Theme Ideas*, she wrote. *Swimming? Bowling? Movie? Video Fun World? Horseback Riding? Chartering a Boat?*

She stared at the last item for a few seconds and then wrote next to it, *Offer to clean all bathrooms for free for entire summer?* Even though her parents had promised her that this year she could have an exotic and unusual birthday party, Lexie still knew their limits. They'd said she could have any kind of party she wanted "within reason." In the Nielsen house "within reason" almost always meant something that didn't cost too much.

Lexie switched over to the right-hand margin and wrote, *Guest List: Lexie Nielsen, Suzy Frankowski, Cheryl Ingebrettson.* Then she stopped and chewed on the end of her pencil. Suzy and Cheryl were two of Lexie's closest friends, but they weren't her best friend. Her best friend was Debby Figenbaum, and normally Debby's name would have been second on the list right under Lexie's. But that wasn't possible this year because Debby wasn't even in town right now. Debby's father was a visiting professor at Stanford University this semester, and the whole Figenbaum family had moved out to California in January. They wouldn't be coming back until the end of June which was almost three whole months away.

It wasn't easy planning your birthday party without

your best friend, Lexie thought glumly. Her eyes roved around the fourth grade classroom, hunting for additional guest list possibilities. She automatically eliminated all the boys, and she barely glanced at Shirley Spitzer or Brooke Stewart, the two girls sitting closest to her. Shirley was overweight and always having trouble with schoolwork, and she went around giggling hysterically whenever anybody in the class teased her. Brooke was a conceited snob who thought that she was better than everybody else just because she wore designer clothes.

Lexie's eyes moved over to the next row and came to rest on Lauren Lindskog. Lauren and Lexie weren't close friends, but they did have quite a few connections. Lauren was in Lexie's scout troop, and she'd invited Lexie to her birthday party last fall. Also, her older sister, Barb, was friends with Faith. Lauren was a quiet kind of person, but when she did say something it was usually pretty smart. Lexie considered for a minute and then added Lauren's name to the list.

When she glanced up from her paper again, she saw Gretchen Dietz smiling at her from two rows away. Lexie didn't know Gretchen very well because she was new, but yesterday Gretchen had called Lexie at home and asked her to come over to her house this afternoon after school. Lexie smiled back at Gretchen. She wrote, *Gretchen Dietz?* at the bottom of her list. Then she drew a thick black line. Five including herself was a good round number, she thought. The fewer guests she invited, the more likely her parents would be to pay for something really different like horseback riding or a trip to an amusement park.

"I like the way Lexie is bent over her paper, concentrating on her work!" Mr. Snyder said from the front of the room. "Have you worked out the number of segments and angles for each figure on the board yet, Lexie?"

Lexie's face grew hot as she quickly covered her paper with her arm. "No, not yet," she mumbled. "I'm still working on it."

She still hadn't figured out the answer five hours later when she met Gretchen Dietz in the front of the room and headed out the classroom door with her.

"Another day over and done with," Gretchen sighed.

"Yeah. But too bad it's only Tuesday!"

"I know what you mean!" Gretchen laughed. "Come on, Lexie, what were you really working on during math this morning? I could see you making all kinds of drawings and lists on your paper."

"I was planning my birthday party," Lexie blurted out. Then she added hastily, "You're invited, of course!"

"Oh, great!" Gretchen said enthusiastically. "What kind of party are you having?"

"I haven't made up my mind. But my parents promised I could do something unusual this year instead of having boring games and ice cream and cake at home. I just can't decide what I want to do."

"My parents hired a magician at my last party before I moved to this neighborhood," Gretchen said. "He was also a ventriloquist, and he was *so* funny! Maybe my mother could give your mother his name."

"Maybe," Lexie said airily. Probably not, she thought to herself. She knew it cost a lot of money to hire a professional magician for a birthday party and she already knew what her parents would say about that. Hiring a magician-ventriloquist would be classified as "not within the family entertainment budget."

"Anyway," Lexie continued, "I'll let you know as soon as I decide about the theme. Or else I'll write it on the invitations."

Before long, the two girls reached Gretchen's big white house on Lake Boulevard. When they stepped inside, they went into a room Gretchen referred to as the "great room." There they found Gretchen's mother stretched out on a thick rose-colored rug in front of the VCR.

"Hi, girls!" she said as she leaned forward to grab the toes of her left foot. "I'm almost finished torturing myself with this exercise tape. If you're hungry, there's a plate of cookies on the kitchen table."

"Okay, Mom." Gretchen headed out of the room and into the kitchen, and Lexie started after her. Then she stopped and turned back to stare at Mrs. Dietz for a few seconds. She knew it was rude, but she just couldn't help herself. Mrs. Dietz was so young and glamorous-looking, it was hard to believe she was anybody's mother! She was small and slim, and she was dressed in a shiny black leotard and purple leg warmers just like a professional aerobics instructor on TV. Her blonde hair was caught up in a terry-cloth headband, but it still fell down around her shoulders in long, fluffy curls. Her face looked something like Gretchen's, which meant that it was delicate and heart-shaped and pretty.

"Hey, Lexie!" Gretchen called. "Did you get lost?"

Lexie shook herself and turned to follow the sound of her friend's voice. She found Gretchen sitting at a round wooden table in the middle of a big blue and white kitchen. Gretchen passed her a plate of cookies, and Lexie helped herself. She took one bite and moaned with pleasure. "Chocolate chip," she sighed. "Soft and chewy, just the way I like them. Where did your mom get them?"

"She made them, of course!" Gretchen said in surprise. She wiped her mouth on a napkin and got to her feet. "Hey, Mom! Can Lexie and I go upstairs and play with your makeup?"

Mrs. Dietz came into the kitchen. She reached for a cookie, and gave Lexie a conspiratorial wink. Lexie stared at the delicate gold and pearl earrings that dangled from her ears.

"It's nice to finally meet you in person, Lexie,"

Gretchen's mother said. "I met your mother at a PTA meeting last month, but I'm not sure she'd remember me."

"Can we play with your makeup, Mom?" Gretchen asked again.

"I guess so. But I was thinking you two might want to help me make dinner instead. I'm just about to get started."

Confused, Lexie glanced at the clock on the wall. It was only three-thirty! Why was Mrs. Dietz starting to cook now? Did the Dietzes eat dinner at four in the afternoon?

"That sounds like fun," Gretchen said enthusiastically. "What are we having?"

"Coq au vin."

This was too much for Lexie. "Wait a minute. You're having cocoa for dinner?"

Mrs. Dietz smiled at her. "It sounds like it, doesn't it? But actually 'coq au vin' is just the French way of saying chicken in wine."

"It's yummy," Gretchen said. "And we'll get to have tastes while we're cooking. What do you want us to do first, Mom?"

For the next hour, Mrs. Dietz had Lexie and Gretchen scurrying around the kitchen, sautéing bacon, chopping onions and mushrooms, and rubbing salt and pepper into a cut-up chicken. Though Lexie's favorite job was blending some butter and flour into a paste

Mrs. Dietz called "beurre manie," the highlight of the afternoon came when it was time to pour a kind of liqueur called cognac all over the chicken.

"Here, Lexie," Mrs. Dietz told her, handing her a box of matches. "Light a match. Then turn your face away and set the cognac on fire."

Lexie gaped at her. She couldn't believe they'd gone to all this trouble getting the chicken ready, only to set the whole thing on fire!

"Go on, Lexie," Gretchen urged. "Wait'll you see what happens. It looks just like fireworks."

Lexie held her breath, lit the match, and tossed it into the red cast-iron pot on the big black stove. Immediately, blue flames shot up around the chicken. Mrs. Dietz shook the pot back and forth for a while until the flames slowly died down.

"That's a way of burning off the alcohol," she explained, as she started pouring red wine over the chicken, "while still keeping the flavor of the cognac."

"It smells really good," Lexie said.

"It's yummy," Gretchen repeated. "Say, Mom, don't you think Lexie should stay for dinner after all this work she's been doing?"

"We'd love to have you, Lexie." Mrs. Dietz started ladling homemade chicken stock out of another pot on the stove. "But of course you'll have to call home for permission."

Lexie glanced up at the clock again, and saw to her

surprise that it was already almost five o'clock. If she left right now, she could get home just in time to avoid getting in trouble. On the family job schedule, it was her night to help with dinner preparation. "I'd like to stay," she told Gretchen's mother, "but I think I'd better go on home. I have to go shopping with my mom tonight right after dinner. We're buying my birthday party invitations."

"That sounds super!" Mrs. Dietz said. "But next time you help us cook, you'll have to promise to stay and eat the fruits of your labors."

"I promise." Lexie gathered up her bookbag, said good-bye to Gretchen, and hurried out the back door. Fifteen minutes later, she walked through the front door of her own house and went through the dining room into the kitchen. She expected to see her mother bustling around cooking something, but instead she found only her father. He was standing in front of the open freezer, busily scraping frost off the top of a warped frozen dinner.

"Do you have any clue as to what this might be, Lexie?" he asked when he saw her. "I can't quite seem to make out what it says on the label."

"I don't have the slightest idea. Where's Mom?"

"Well, she just called to say she's running late again," Mr. Nielsen explained. "Apparently she had a long meeting with her advisor in St. Paul this afternoon, and then she had to stop by somewhere and pick up some kind of petition about Penelope Dove, so she suggested we pop something into the microwave for dinner. Faith's off baby-sitting for the Larsens tonight and Daniel's working at McD again, so it's just you and me for the time being. We can spend the entire mealtime swapping riddles with no one around to tell us how corny we are." He scraped another layer of frost off the carton in his hand. "Aha! I can read it now. It's flash-frozen tofu lasagna. How does that sound to you?"

Lexie didn't say anything. As she stood there staring at her father in front of the freezer, she was really seeing Mrs. Dietz and Gretchen, a plate of homemade chocolate chip cookies, and a potful of simmering coq au vin.

"What do you say, Lexerino?" Mr. Nielsen's head was back inside the freezer. "Could you stomach the tofu, or would you rather go for this Mexican broccoli and green bean fiesta I've just unearthed?"

Lexie still didn't say anything, and Mr. Nielsen backed out of the freezer and looked at her. "Lexie? Are you listening to me? I'm asking you what you'd like to have for dinner tonight."

Lexie shook her head and dropped her backpack on the floor. "Make whatever you want," she said as she turned around and stomped out of the kitchen. "I'm not hungry."

FOUR

When Lexie came back into the kitchen a few minutes later, her father was carefully taking two steaming cartons out of the microwave. "I made both the lasagna and the fiesta," he said. "You can have first pick."

"I think I'll make myself a sandwich again." Lexie crossed over to the refrigerator.

"Well, I think I'll opt for the lasagna, then," Mr. Nielsen said as he carried one carton over to the table. "But if you change your mind and decide you want it, I'll be happy to trade."

When Lexie had finished making her peanut butter and jelly, the two of them sat down at the kitchen table and started eating. Mr. Nielsen took one bite of his tofu lasagna, made a face, and carefully put down his fork. "This dinner puts me in mind of an inky pinky."

Lexie stopped chewing. An inky pinky was a riddle with two rhyming words for its answer. They could be very hard, but she loved trying to answer them.

"Let's see," her father began thoughtfully. "I have to think of a good way of phrasing the question. All right, I have it: What is an inky pinky for bean curd that is impossible to masticate?"

"No fair! I don't know what masticate means."

"It means to grind up with your teeth."

"Okay." Lexie took a swallow of milk and considered. The bean curd part of the answer was obviously "tofu." And masticate probably was "chew." So that gave her "chew tofu." "I've got it!" Lexie cried. "The answer is 'no chew tofu!' "

"Very good, kiddo." Her father got to his feet and reached for the peanut butter jar. "I believe I'll join you in a sandwich."

Lexie glanced over at her father's lasagna carton. "I have an even better inky pinky about your dinner," she said. "What is bean curd that looks like stuff you get on your feet?"

Her father frowned. "Lexie . . . ," he began.

"The answer is 'tofu toe-goo!' "

"Lexie, that is in very poor taste."

"Well, so was your tofu lasagna," Lexie pointed out.

Mr. Nielsen shrugged and made a face at her. "I'll concede the point," he said, sitting down at the table. He'd just taken his first bite out of his sandwich when Mrs. Nielsen burst through the door. "Oh, I'm glad you went ahead and started without me," she said when she saw them. "I just have time for a quick sandwich myself, and then I have to go back out again. Apparently there was some kind of mix-up about the petition for getting Penelope on the ballot, and they came up twenty signatures short. It seems nobody covered the Lake Calhoun neighborhood, so I said I'd go door to door over there tonight and see if I can get the names they need."

Lexie opened her mouth to ask about buying her birthday party invitations, but before she had a chance to say anything, Mr. Nielsen put down his sandwich and drummed his fingertips on the table. "Barbara," he said, "I have a Community Welfare Council board meeting tonight. And I know I didn't forget to tell you about this one. It's been on the calendar for a month."

Mrs. Nielsen put her pile of books and papers on the table. "Oh, dear," she said. "You're right. I'm sorry, Frank. I forgot all about it." She reached for a piece of bread and started spreading peanut butter on it. "Do you suppose Faith and Lexie could stay home together two nights in a row?"

"Faith's already baby-sitting for the Larsens," Lexie

reminded her. "And Daniel's working again. And Karen doesn't get home until tomorrow afternoon." Yesterday she might have suggested staying home by herself tonight. But after last night she didn't feel like it. Being alone in the big dark house with the memory of the old sea captain was the last thing on earth she felt like doing.

"Oh, dear," Mrs. Nielsen said again. She started screwing the cap off the jelly jar, but then she stopped and looked at Lexie. "Well, if you don't want to be by yourself all evening, honey, I guess you'll just have to come help me gather signatures for Penelope Dove," she said. "I'm sure it won't take us that long. And besides it'll be good hands-on, educational experience for you. You'll get to see how the American political process operates right down at the grass roots level!"

Whoopee, Lexie thought. But when she looked at Mrs. Nielsen's flushed, enthusiastic face, she forgot all about making a sarcastic comment. Instead, her attention was caught by her mother's baby-fine, light brown hair. As usual, it was bunched up and jumbled into a careless bun at the back of her head. In the morning, the bun didn't look too bad, but as the day went on, more and more pieces of it escaped. By evening, at least half of Mrs. Nielsen's hair was floating out in wispy feathers around her face.

"Mom, did you ever think about getting a perm?" Lexie asked.

Mrs. Nielsen laughed. "Where did that question come from?" she asked. She took a few bites out of her sandwich and then reached for her totebag. "As a matter of fact I did get a perm once a long time ago. As I recall, it was a total disaster, right, Frank?"

"I refuse to comment on the grounds it might tend to incriminate me," Mr. Nielsen said solemnly.

"Come on, Lexie," her mother said. "We'd better get going before it gets too late to knock on people's doors."

Lexie grabbed her latest library book from the counter and followed her mother outside to where the station wagon was parked in the driveway. She planned to stay in the car and read until it was time to go back home, but when they reached the Lake Calhoun neighborhood, Mrs. Nielsen made her get out.

"I won't be able to concentrate on what I'm doing if I'm worrying about you sitting all alone in the car, Lexie. And besides, it won't hurt you to see what gathering names on a petition is like. Who knows? Maybe someday you'll be circulating a petition about something!"

"I doubt it," Lexie said. She'd never been able to understand how her mother could get so worked up about politics and all her other causes. She just couldn't imagine herself ever caring so intensely about things that seemed so dry and boring.

She trailed her mother up the walk to the first house

on the block. "Hello, my name is Barbara Nielsen," Mrs. Nielsen told the man who answered the knock. "And I'm here collecting signatures for a petition to get Penelope Dove on the ballot for the next school board election. Have you had a chance to hear anything about Ms. Dove and her stand on the issues?"

"Yeah, I've heard about her!" the man snarled. "I've heard she's a communist!" He slammed the door in their faces.

Surprised, Mrs. Nielsen stepped backward and almost fell off the edge of the sidewalk. "Well!" she said as she clutched Lexie's arm for support. "Of all the ignorant, bigoted, close-minded . . ." She looked at Lexie and made a wry face. "There's your first lesson in politics, Lex! It takes all kinds to make a world."

The next person on the street was more polite. She was an older lady with gray hair who invited them in for tea and cookies, which, to Lexie's disappointment, her mother politely refused. "I don't have any children in school anymore," the woman explained in a soft voice. "So I don't get involved in the school board issues."

"I can certainly understand that," Lexie's mother said. "But don't you feel as if the whole community has a responsibility for one another's children? After all, they do say our children are our future. And Penelope Dove wants to help improve all the schools in the city.

Surely, in the long run, improving the schools will help improve society as a whole?"

The woman smiled at Lexie's mother and gave Lexie a wink. "Your mommy makes a pretty persuasive argument, doesn't she, young lady?" she said. "Maybe she's the one who ought to be running for something!" She took the pen and wrote her name at the bottom of the petition. "After all, I guess it can't hurt to help get somebody's name on the ballot. It doesn't mean I have to vote for her."

"You're absolutely right about that." Mrs. Nielsen thanked the woman, and she and Lexie moved on to the next house on the block and then on to the next. For the next two hours, Lexie listened to her mother talk to people about an endless number of complicated issues facing the school board. At first, she tried to listen, but soon she became bored and bleary-eyed with exhaustion. By the time they finally managed to collect the twenty signatures they needed, all she wanted to do was crawl in bed and close her eyes.

"Mom, why are you doing all this work?" she asked wearily when they were back in the car and on their way home. "What in the world is so great about this Penelope Dove person?"

"Well, I guess the main thing I like about her is that she really does seem to care about all the schools in town, Lexie. For instance, she says she wants to get special support for the Water Street School because it's so overcrowded and rundown. They need extra funds and more support staff over there, but nobody is doing anything about it."

"But the Water Street School is way across town from us, Mom. I don't even go to school there."

"Of course you don't. And Penelope Dove's children don't, either. But even so she feels a responsibility for the children who *do* go there. That's not so hard to understand, is it?"

"I guess not," Lexie said slowly. "But half the people you talked to tonight seemed to think Penelope is pretty weird."

"Well, just between you and me, Lexie, Penelope *can* seem a little strange when you meet her in person or see her on TV. She's very intense, and she sometimes comes across as a bit of a fanatic. I'm afraid it turns people off. But her heart's in the right place, and that's what really matters."

Lexie started to say something else about Penelope Dove, but at that moment, they drove past the Party Shop. "Mom!" she cried. "We never bought my birthday invitations. Let's stop and see if the store's still open."

Her mother peered at the clock on the dashboard. "It can't possibly be open, honey," she said. "It's almost nine-thirty already."

"Well, when are we going to buy them then, Mom?"

Lexie wailed. "I have to get them in the mail right away!"

"That's something I need to talk to you about, Lex. I never got a chance to finish telling you, but yesterday I ran into one of the other mothers from your school in Exotic Appetizers, and it seems her daughter is in your class, and she's planning to have her birthday party at the exact same time we were planning to have yours. In fact, she's already sent out her invitations. Yours should be coming in the mail this week."

Lexie sat up and stared at her mother in consternation. "Maybe we didn't invite all the same kids. I'm only inviting a few."

"Believe it or not, according to her mother, this girl invited every single child in your class, including all the boys!"

"Just who is this girl, anyway, Mom? She can't be one of my friends, or I already would have heard about her party."

"I can't remember her first name, but her mother's name was Carolyn Spitzer."

"Spitzer!" Lexie repeated. "That must have been Shirley Spitzer's mother." She leaned back against the seat again and relaxed in the dark. "In that case, we don't really have a problem."

"I'm glad to hear it, Lexie, but why not? You know how we hassled around in circles with the calendar last week. We're going to be out of town the weekend after your birthday, so we can't have your party a week late. And Daddy and I are both tied up all day on Sunday the 20th, so we can't have it the day after, either. Besides which, you're the one who insisted you had to have your party on Saturday the 19th because that was your actual birthday. So please tell me why we don't have a conflict with Shirley."

"Because nobody will go to her party, Mom. At least none of my friends will. So I can just go ahead and invite them anyway."

Lexie's mother didn't say anything for a long moment, and Lexie began to think the birthday party discussion was over and done with. But after a while, Mrs. Nielsen spoke in a quiet voice. "Would you mind telling me exactly why it is that nobody will go to Shirley's party, Lexie?"

"Oh, well, Shirley's just not that popular, I guess," Lexie said casually. "You know, she's kind of fat and dumb, and the kids always make fun of her and everything. I think she might even be old enough to be in fifth grade already—but she can hardly even handle fourth grade!"

"Uh-huh," Mrs. Nielsen said slowly. "And am I to assume that you are one of the kids who's participated in making fun of Shirley?"

Uh-oh, Lexie thought to herself. From the tone of her mother's voice, she immediately recognized that she'd made a serious blunder. Why had she spoken about Shirley Spitzer like that? It was just the kind of mean talking that drove her mother crazy!

"Of course *I* don't make fun of Shirley, Mom," she said earnestly. "It's mostly the boys like Stevie Crawford and Kippy Meyer who do it. You know how rude they are." As she spoke, she felt a small pang of guilt. While it was true she'd never actually teased Shirley to her face, she'd certainly made fun of her behind her back. And once or twice she'd stood around giggling when other kids made fun of her. "But anyway, Mom, Shirley doesn't seem to mind being teased at all. I told you she just laughs when the kids pick on her. She thinks it's funny!"

"Uh-huh," Mrs. Nielsen said again. "Well, be that as it may, Lexie, I think you should know that despite what you think, *I* still think we *do* have a problem about the birthday parties—in fact, I now believe it's an even bigger problem than I'd first realized." She was quiet for another minute. "When the party conflict came up in Exotic Appetizers last night, I thought Mrs. Spitzer seemed a little upset, and I couldn't figure out why. But now I understand why she was so concerned. She must be very worried about Shirley if the other kids are picking on her."

"I suppose," Lexie mumbled.

"Anyway, I went ahead and invited Mrs. Spitzer to our house for coffee, and she and Shirley are coming over tomorrow after school. Maybe if you two kids put your heads together you might be able to come up with a solution about the parties."

Now it was Lexie's turn to be quiet. She was so shocked she couldn't think of anything to say. When she finally did speak, her voice was shaky and tearful. "Mom," she wavered, "just exactly what kind of solution are you suggesting? Do you want me to say I'll join up with Shirley and have one great big jolly party together with her or something?"

"I'm not making any suggestions, Lexie. I'm just hoping you and Shirley will be able to work something out together—something that will make both of you feel happy about your birthdays."

"Well, I don't care what Shirley wants!" Lexie screamed, bursting into tears. "I care about what *I* want! You promised me I could have a *good* party this year, for the first time ever! It was supposed to be the best party I've ever had—the perfect party I've been dreaming about my whole life long! But now you're trying to make me change all my plans—just to suit Shirley Spitzer. Well, I won't do it! If the only way I can have a party is to share it with somebody as weird as Shirley Spitzer, then I won't have a party at all!"

FIVE

When Lexie came into the kitchen the next morning, she found Faith sitting at the table by herself, eating a bowl of cereal and gloomily studying the back of the Cheerios box. Lexie opened the refrigerator and took the last English muffin out of its package. She put it into the toaster oven and went over to look in the cupboard.

"Where's the peanut butter?"

"How should I know?" Faith snapped. "You're the peanut butter addict around here."

Lexie straightened up and turned around to scowl at her sister. "Aren't *we* charming this morning!" she said. "Did something happen to make you even crabbier than usual?"

"If you must know, I'm in a bad mood because Karen's coming home today, and that means I have to move back in with piggy little you tonight."

"Oh, big deal," Lexie said. "You'd use any excuse to start pouting. I have a *real* problem, but you don't see me going around being rude to everybody, do you?" She spotted the peanut butter jar still sitting on the counter where she'd left it the night before. As she picked it up, Daniel limped into the kitchen and took the Wheaties box out of the cupboard. He'd twisted his ankle at softball practice the day before yesterday, which accounted for the step-*thud* he'd made coming up the stairs two nights before.

"Seen any old sea captains lately, you two?" he asked. Though Faith and Lexie had told Daniel about watching *Chiller Theater,* they'd begged him not to tell their parents, and he'd finally said he wouldn't. So far he'd been true to his word, but that hadn't stopped him from torturing his sisters about the sea captain whenever he was alone with them.

"You still smell like french fries," Faith sweetly informed him from behind the Cheerios box.

"I know. I take two showers every night, but it doesn't help." He poured some Wheaties into a bowl and opened the refrigerator. "Geez!" he exclaimed as he looked inside. "There's no milk left! Doesn't Mom *ever* go to the store anymore? What am I supposed to have for breakfast?"

Faith looked guiltily at the last few drops of milk sitting in the bottom of her bowl. "I guess you could have half my English muffin," Lexie said. "But it's already got peanut butter on it."

"No, thanks." Daniel moved away from the refrigerator and started rummaging through the cupboard where he finally discovered a hidden box of granola bars. "I guess I'll just eat these," he said, limping back out of the kitchen.

"Do you suppose he's going to eat all of them?" Lexie wondered as she watched him leave. "That was a brand-new box!"

"Jocks need their energy," Faith said. "So, anyway, what's this terrible problem of yours that you're facing with such brave cheerfulness?"

Lexie sat down with her muffin and eyed her sister across the table. More often than not when she told Faith about a problem, Faith made fun of her and said her concerns were too babyish to be considered real problems. But every now and then, if she could get Faith's attention, her sister managed to come up with a piece of good advice.

Lexie decided her situation was desperate enough to warrant taking a chance on being ridiculed. "As usual," she said through a mouthful of muffin, "my problem is Mom. She found out this weird girl Shirley invited every single person in our class to a birthday party on the exact same date I'm having mine! I said I'd just go ahead and invite my friends anyway and let them do what they wanted. But do you think Mom the Good would let me do that? *Noooo!* She's insisting that Shirley and I have to 'put our heads together' and 'work out a solution.' I just know Mom wants us to have one big party together or something."

Lexie stopped talking long enough to take another bite of breakfast. Then she continued ranting on about her mother and the party for several more minutes. Faith finally started banging the side of her cereal bowl with her spoon. "All *right,* Lexie! I get the picture. Now stop babbling for a second so I can think. Hmmm." She drummed her fingers on the tabletop. "Obviously, the simplest solution is for you to change the date of your party."

"Well, of course I already thought of that, Faith. But Saturday is really the only day I can have it. Mom showed me the family calendar, and practically every single other day already has something written on it. Besides, Saturday is the 19th, and it's my real birthday. For once in my life, I'd like to have my party on my actual birthday! It's almost never happened before."

"Hmmm," Faith said again. "Well, have you considered getting this Shirley person to change the date of her party?"

"That's it, Faith!" Lexie cried. "You're a genius! Why didn't I think of that? All I have to do is ask Shirley to change her party around. Then my problems will be solved!"

"You hope they will be," Faith said. "Remember, Shirley hasn't agreed to do it yet. And you know how Mom is. She may not want to let you take the easy way out like that, particularly if Shirley is some kind of kid with problems." She slurped up her last drop of milk and got to her feet. "What's Shirley like anyway? What's so weird about her?"

Lexie chewed on another bite of English muffin. "Well, everybody always makes fun of her," she said thoughtfully, "but to tell you the truth I'm not sure any of the kids actually *know* Shirley. I mean, we know she wears glasses and she's overweight and she can't read very well. And she goes around giggling all the time. But that's about it."

"Well, I know you'll say I'm being a goody-goody, but don't you think you might at least try to find out what she's really like? If you're lucky maybe she'll turn out not to be so bad. And you say she already invited everybody in your class. So if you end up having one big party, all those kids will be coming to your party, too, and that means you'll get more presents. That should appeal to the Lexie I know and love."

"I know you won't believe me, Faith, but I really don't care that much about getting presents anymore. What I do care about is having a good party, and Mom and Daddy promised me that this year I could have an extraordinary *different* kind of party for once. If I have to invite twenty-two kids, that will be impossible! We'll be stuck here doing the same old stuff—like playing pin-the-tail-on-the-donkey and musical chairs."

Faith started to make a comment, but just then Mrs. Nielsen hurried into the kitchen. She looked at the clock radio and made an exclamation of dismay. "I don't even have five minutes for breakfast! I hope my stomach doesn't growl during my personality disorder seminar." She shot Lexie a sideways glance. "If we leave right now, Lex, I just have time to drop you off at school on my way to the U."

"No, thank you, Mother," Lexie said formally. "I prefer to walk this morning."

"Lexie . . ." Mrs. Nielsen began.

"In fact, I think I'd better get going right now," Lexie continued in the same tone. "I don't wish to be tardy." Without even saying good-bye, she left the kitchen, picked up her bookbag in the living room, and walked out the door of the house. On the front steps, she experienced a moment of guilt over being so mean to her mother, but she decided not to let it bother her. She felt that her sudden exit made the perfect dramatic statement of how she felt about Mrs. Nielsen's interference with her birthday party.

When she got to school, Lexie's already bad mood continued to grow steadily worse. First, Mr. Snyder asked her to turn in all her overdue math homework by the end of the week *or else*. Then during recess Cheryl Ingebrettson and Suzy Frankowski asked her to go to the park with them that afternoon after school. She automatically said yes, but then remembered that Shirley Spitzer and her mother were coming over to her house. For an instant, she almost pretended she'd forgotten all about it, but then she decided she probably couldn't get away with it. Unhappily, she forced herself to tell Cheryl and Suzy she couldn't go with them after all. After school, as she watched her friends cross Fiftieth Street and head for the park, she felt consumed with self-pity. By the time she reached home, she was in a silent rage at the world.

When she walked through the front door, the first thing she saw was her oldest sister Karen's suitcase sitting in the middle of the floor. "Little Lexie-pooh!" Karen screamed, bouncing in from the kitchen. "Did we miss our big siss-siss?"

For the moment, Lexie forgot her bad mood. In spite of the fact that she usually despised being talked to in baby talk, she was astonished to discover she was actually quite happy to see Karen again. She walked across the room and let her sister plant a big sloppy kiss on the middle of her forehead.

"Hi, Karen," she said. "How was your trip?"

"Oh, Lexie, it was absolutely, unbelievably fantastic. I just can't wait to go away to college. All three places I visited were just super!"

Lexie looked at Karen's excited face and felt a twinge of envy. It must be wonderful, she thought, to be almost grown-up and able to make your own decisions about an important issue like picking out the college you wanted to go to.

"Which one did you like best?"

"Well, I had a great time at St. Torvald's and Darnell. But the place I really truly adored was Brandham."

"So is that where you're going to go?"

"Well, I certainly hope so, Lex-Lex. But you know how Mom and Daddy are. The place is astronomically expensive so of course I'd have to qualify for a scholarship before they'd let me go there."

Lexie didn't have the slightest idea of what a scholarship was, but before she had a chance to ask, Mrs. Nielsen came through the front door. All at once, Lexie's almost forgotten bad mood flooded back in full force. Without another word to either her sister or her mother, she turned around and stomped up the stairs to her room.

She was sitting on her unmade bed staring out the window when a quiet little knock sounded on her door.

Bracing herself for a new confrontation with her mother, she yelled, "I can't stop you so you might as well come in!"

The door opened, and Shirley Spitzer walked in. She stopped short and stared around the cluttered room. "Wow!" she said in disbelief. "I thought *my* room was messy!"

"If you don't like it, you can leave," Lexie said nastily.

Shirley folded her arms across her chest. "Don't you think that's just what I *want* to do?" she asked. "But my mother's standing guard with your mother downstairs. She won't let me leave until we figure out what to do about our birthday parties."

"Oh, geez," Lexie said. "We're going to be stuck here all afternoon!"

"I don't see why," Shirley said shortly. "I sent my invitations out first. So you just have to switch your party around to a different time."

"I can't. My family's so busy, that's the only day they can squeeze it in. Can you change yours?"

"I suppose I could, but I don't see why I should. I already sent out all my invitations."

"Well, maybe you could call everybody up and tell them you're having the party on a different day or something."

"I don't want to. I'd rather forget about the whole thing. The truth is, I don't want to have a birthday party at all. I wouldn't even be having one, but my mother's making me do it!"

Lexie stared in surprise. To her, a birthday party was the highlight of the year. As soon as one of Lexie's parties was over, she started planning her next one. She couldn't imagine somebody not wanting to have a birthday party. "That's unbelievable," she said slowly.

"I know," Shirley said. "My mother is the pushiest, bossiest person in the world."

"Ha!" Lexie said. "I can see you don't know *my* mother very well. But that's not what I meant. I meant it was unbelievable that you don't want to have a birthday party."

"Well, think about it," Shirley said. "Would you want one if you were me?"

Lexie couldn't think of anything to say. She darted a look at Shirley's eyes behind their thick glasses but then immediately felt compelled to look away again. In that short glance, something in Shirley's expression had communicated itself to Lexie, and it wasn't pleasant. For a split second, Lexie felt almost as if she'd been possessed by Shirley, just the way the husband in *Chiller Theater* had been possessed by the old sea captain. Lexie now knew why Shirley didn't want to have a party.

It's not my fault! she thought desperately. *It's not my fault about Shirley and the other kids at school!* But saying this to herself didn't make her feel any better.

She still didn't want to look Shirley in the eye, and for some reason, she felt guilty and ashamed about it. She didn't know exactly why she felt that way, but she knew she didn't like it. She made a long, intensive study of a pile of dirty socks on the floor next to her bed. Then she cleared her throat.

"Do you want to see this special place I have?" she asked. "It's kind of scary getting there, but after that it's really great."

"I guess so," Shirley said doubtfully. "Where is it?"

Lexie got off the bed and left the room. In the upstairs hallway, she opened a glass door that led out onto an open balcony sun porch that overlooked the backyard.

"Is this your special place?" Shirley asked, following her outside.

"No. The roof is my special place." Lexie pointed around the corner of the sun porch. "The very top is almost perfectly flat, but we have to climb up that steep part over there to get up to it."

Shirley looked over at the slanted rooftop next to the sun porch, and her eyes narrowed. Lexie remembered how uncoordinated Shirley was at all the sports events at school. "Maybe it's not such a good idea after all," she began hastily. "We could just stay right here on the porch instead."

"No," Shirley said firmly. "I want to do it. But you'd better go first. If I go first and fall on you, you'll get squashed."

Lexie wasn't sure if Shirley was talking about being fat or clumsy, but either way she wasn't sure what to say to her. "Let's go at the same time," she finally suggested. "That way, if either one of us slips, the other one can go tell our moms what happened."

Without another word, Shirley hoisted her pudgy legs over the railing and onto the shingles. Lexie climbed after her, and the two of them scrambled up the side of the roof on all fours. By the time they reached the top of the house, they were both breathing hard.

"Wow," Shirley gasped as she sat down on the flat green shingled area of the roof. "It *is* really great up here. You can see all over."

Lexie pointed a finger. "See that gray house over there? That's Kippy Meyer's house. One time I brought binoculars up here, and I could see right into his room."

"Ugh!" Shirley said vehemently. "Was there green slime all over the walls?"

Surprised, Lexie stared at Shirley's round face. "I thought you liked Kippy Meyer! You laugh at everything he says to you at school."

"Well, what am I supposed to do? Go around crying all the time? What do you think Kippy would have to say about that?"

For the second time that afternoon, Lexie discovered she couldn't meet Shirley's eyes. Instead she flopped over onto her stomach and pointed down at the street below. "I like to watch the people walking around down there," she said. "They look even smaller than my old dollhouse people."

Shirley turned over onto her stomach and gazed down at the street. "Do you come up here with any of your friends?" she asked. "Like Debby or Cheryl or Suzy? Or that new girl Gretchen Dietz?"

Lexie was surprised that Shirley knew exactly who all her friends were. "Now that you mention it," she said, "I don't think I've ever brought anybody else up here at all. The problem is, I'm not even really allowed to be on the roof. My sister, Karen, discovered this flat part a few years ago, and started coming up here to sunbathe. When my mom found out about it, she really freaked out about how dangerous it was."

"My mom would have given her a lecture on skin cancer."

Lexie giggled. "I think our moms are a lot alike."

"You're right," Shirley laughed. "Lucky us." She was quiet for a long moment. "I've been thinking, Lexie," she announced suddenly. "And I guess maybe I can change my party to a different day after all. I'll just send out new invitations, and you can have your party on the 19th after all."

Lexie's mouth dropped open. "Wow, Shirley!" she exclaimed. "Wow. That's really nice of you. Thanks a lot. That's just perfect." *Hurray!* she told herself. Everything was solved. The perfect party could still happen. And it had all been so simple!

She stretched out and prepared for a warm, happy glow to spread over her body. But, though she waited several long seconds, to her dismay, the feeling never came. Instead, she gradually became aware of an annoying tightening sensation deep inside her chest. She frowned and took a deep breath, but the tightness didn't go away. If anything, it seemed to be getting worse.

Shirley hauled herself up to a kneeling position. "I guess we should go down and tell our moms we worked things out," she said. She gave her familiar high-pitched giggle. "They'll be so happy."

Lexie nodded but didn't make any move to stand up. She was lost in thought, trying to figure out why she felt so strange. She just couldn't understand it. Here she'd gotten exactly what she'd been hoping for. She could plan any kind of theme she wanted. She could invite whoever she wanted. And she could have her party when she wanted. Shirley had just solved everything. It had been easy. Easy.

Easy for *you*, Lexie, a small voice inside her said. But what about Shirley?

The tightness in Lexie's chest increased, and she almost groaned out loud. She took another deep breath and shot a sideways glance at Shirley, who was staring over in the direction of Kippy Meyer's window. The other girl's round face was expressionless, but once again, Lexie felt she understood at least a little bit of what she was feeling.

Suddenly, a voice broke into the silence on the roof-top. "I have a different idea," it said. "Instead of you switching your party around, what if we joined up together and had one big party?" With a start, Lexie realized *she* was the one doing the talking! She blinked and swallowed hard.

Shirley stared at her in disbelief. "You're joking, right?" she said.

Lexie slowly shook her head. "No," she heard her voice say in a firm, positive tone. "I'm serious." As she answered, she realized her voice was speaking the truth. She really was serious about sharing her party with Shirley! "If it's okay with you, that is," she added.

"Well, I hadn't really thought about it," Shirley said. "But I guess it's okay. Anyway, I know my mom will be thrilled."

"Mine, too," Lexie laughed. She breathed again and realized the tightness had completely left her chest. "So that part's settled. Now all we have to do is decide what kind of party we want. Let's try to think of something really unusual. If only there didn't have to be so many kids coming!"

She started to ask Shirley why she'd invited their entire class, but she stopped herself just in time. With another flash of insight, she understood why Shirley had asked all the kids. She'd probably figured that if she invited *everybody* at least a few kids might actually have shown up.

She cleared her throat and went on. "Let's see. We can't take all those kids anyplace. It would cost too much."

"And we'd have to hire a bus," Shirley pointed out.

"Right. So we're stuck with one of our houses. What kind of interesting thing can we do at home? Would your parents want to hire a clown or a magician or somebody?"

"I don't think so," Shirley said. "My mom and dad are the cheapest people in the world."

"Ha!" Lexie said. "*Nobody's* cheaper than my mom and dad!" She picked at the warm grainy green surface of a shingle. "I just wish we could think of something *original* to do at the party. You know—something stupefyingly stupendous that nobody's ever done before."

Shirley started pacing back and forth on the roof. "Why do you care so much about what we do at this dumb party, Lexie? I don't see why we have to do anything besides have a birthday cake! Why are you so worried about keeping everybody entertained? Why can't the kids keep themselves entertained? Why are you making such a big deal out of this and . . ."

"Shirley, stop right there!" Lexie interrupted sharply.

Shirley stopped in her tracks and stared at her. "What's the matter? Am I getting too close to the edge of the roof?"

"Well, now that you mention it, maybe you are, but

that wasn't why I told you to stop. I wanted you to stop talking so I could think about what you said."

"What do you mean? What did I say?"

"You said, 'Why can't the kids keep themselves entertained?' And I think you've just come up with the perfect idea for a really fantastic birthday party theme!"

Six

On their way down to the computer in the basement, Shirley and Lexie passed their mothers, who were drinking coffee in the kitchen. As the girls hurried by the table, Mrs. Nielsen put down her blue and white ceramic mug, and stared at them.

"Lexie," she began, "what . . . ?"

"We can't talk now, Mom. We'll tell you what we're doing when we're finished."

Half an hour later, she and Shirley brought a party invitation back upstairs. This is what it looked like.

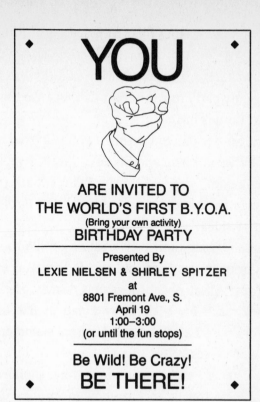

YOU

ARE INVITED TO
THE WORLD'S FIRST B.Y.O.A.
(Bring your own activity)
BIRTHDAY PARTY

Presented By
LEXIE NIELSEN & SHIRLEY SPITZER
at
8801 Fremont Ave., S.
April 19
1:00–3:00
(or until the fun stops)

Be Wild! Be Crazy!
BE THERE!

Lexie put the invitation on the table in front of her mother's coffee mug. Mrs. Spitzer leaned over so she could see it, too. "Hmm," she said. "I'm not sure I understand this, girls. What exactly does this B.Y.O.A. mean?"

"It means that each kid is supposed to be in charge of some kind of activity for the party," Lexie explained. "They could bring games or just have a good idea or whatever they want."

"I see," Shirley's mother said. "A joint party with

the children bringing their own activities! I think it's a lovely plan!"

"It was Lexie's idea," Shirley said. "I was going to change my party to a different day, but she thought we should do this instead."

Mrs. Spitzer blinked in surprise. She looked back and forth between Lexie and Shirley. "Well, I want you to know, Lexie," she said slowly, "that I think you are a very creative thinker. And I'm absolutely *thrilled* about this party idea!"

Remembering their conversation on the roof, Lexie and Shirley both smiled and avoided meeting each other's eyes. All at once, to Lexie's dismay, she saw her mother reach for a tissue and dab at her tear-filled eyes. "L . . . Lexie," Mrs. Nielsen stammered in a strangled voice. "S . . . such a v . . . v . . . validation . . . s . . . s . . . such a nurturing, supportive gesture, I almost can't vocalize how much I . . ."

"*Mom!*" Lexie's cheeks flamed with embarrassment. "Mom!" She searched desperately for something else to say. "You . . . you absolutely *have* to do something about that cold! Your eyes are watering! And you sound like you're running a fever!"

"I have some aspirin in my purse if you need it, Barbara," Mrs. Spitzer said. "But getting back to the invitations, I do have two suggestions to make. You girls need to put in a phone number for responses. And you need to say something about canceling the invitations Shirley already sent out."

"We could put in a little note at the bottom of the page about that," Lexie suggested.

"Good idea," Shirley's mother said. "And then you'd better get the invitations into the mail. The party's only a week and a half away." She looked up at Lexie's mother, who was still wiping at her eyes with her moist tissue. "Are you sure you don't mind having the party at your house, Barbara?"

"Oh, no, I don't mind! Frank and I have been putting on birthday parties for so many years, we're just about ready to turn professional." She turned toward Lexie. "Honey, when you finish printing out the invitations, you'll find envelopes and a roll of stamps in the desk in the living room."

Shirley and Lexie went back down into the basement where they spent the rest of the afternoon printing out the invitations and stuffing them into stamped, addressed envelopes. By the time they finished working, it was almost dinnertime. They'd just licked the last envelope when Mrs. Spitzer came downstairs to get Shirley. Shirley promised to mail the invitations on the way home that night.

When Lexie walked back up into the kitchen, her mother was pawing through the cupboard shelves. "Cornstarch," she muttered as she pushed around boxes. "Baking soda. Spanish olives. Anchovies. Confectioner's sugar. Marinated artichoke hearts."

"What are you doing, Mom?"

Mrs. Nielsen jumped in surprise and whirled around. "You scared me, Lexie!" She turned back toward the cupboard. "I'm just trying to find something we can eat for dinner."

"You don't have a meeting tonight?"

"Lexie, contrary to what you and the rest of the family may think, I don't have a meeting every single night! But I'll admit I've been too busy to go to the store, and we don't seem to have a thing on hand. Do you think everybody would mind eating Cream of Wheat for dinner?"

"I don't mind. But Faith hates it. She says it reminds her of eating wallpaper paste."

"I wonder when she last ate wallpaper paste," Mrs. Nielsen mused.

Just then, the back door opened and Mr. Nielsen came in staggering under the weight of a big brown bag. "I brought takeout from the new Thai restaurant," he said.

"You're a lifesaver, Frank!" Mrs. Nielsen exclaimed. "Extravagant, but still a lifesaver. How did you know we'd need takeout tonight?"

"Well, I just assumed you wouldn't have made it to the store yet. And I thought you might be rushing out the door to a meeting."

"You sound just like Lexie!" Mrs. Nielsen complained. "Why is everybody else allowed to have commitments but me? And why am I the only person in the family considered capable of going to the supermarket?" She moved closer to her husband and sniffed the contents of the brown bag. "Mmmm, that smells much more interesting than Cream of Wheat!"

Lexie, who was also sniffing the bag, wrinkled her nose suspiciously. "What exactly *is* Thai food, Daddy?"

"Food from Thailand, naturally."

"But I mean what is it?"

"Ah. Well, they had an enormous menu, and it was difficult to choose, but I finally settled on sliced pork with garlic and mushrooms marinated in coconut milk, and scallops with lemon grass and chili peppers."

An exaggerated expression of disgust crossed Lexie's face. Without saying a word, she headed for the cupboard and took out the peanut butter jar. Mr. Nielsen shook his head at her and then carried the bag of Thai food into the dining room. Mrs. Nielsen got out some plates and started after him, but then she stopped and turned around.

"Lexie," she said quietly. "This afternoon . . ."

Mrs. Nielsen paused. Lexie was concentrating on the delicate art of spreading the thickest possible layer of jelly onto a piece of bread without slopping over the sides, but she got ready to hear something about the maturation of her complex problem-solving abilities.

When her mother remained silent, Lexie finally looked up from her sandwich and met her gaze. Only then did Mrs. Nielsen continue speaking.

"This afternoon, Lexie," she said again, "you had an easy way out, but you didn't take it. Instead, you did a very nice thing. I know I got a little carried away trying to express how I felt about it. But this is what I really wanted to say: I'm very proud of you."

Instead of answering her mother, Lexie simply smiled, shrugged, and bent back over her sandwich. But as she reached for her knife and scraped another glob of jelly from the bottom of the jelly jar, she finally felt the warm happy glow she'd been waiting for all afternoon. It felt good to earn a genuine compliment, she told herself. And it felt even better when she could actually understand what her mother was talking about!

SEVEN

Unfortunately, the warm glow didn't last very long. By the time she'd joined the rest of the family at the dinner table, Lexie was already starting to have second thoughts about sharing her party with Shirley. True, she told herself, she'd done the Right Thing. She'd made Shirley happy. She'd made Shirley's mother happy. And her own parents would probably nominate her for the Child's Hall of Fame.

But what about the other kids at school? They all thought Shirley Spitzer was weird. When they heard

Lexie was sharing a party with her, wouldn't they assume that Lexie had become weird, too? Even Lexie's friend Cheryl Ingebrettson, one of the nicest people in the world, had made some comments about Shirley. What would she say when she heard Lexie was having a party with her? What would Gretchen Dietz say? What would *Kippy Meyer* say?

She had a lot of time to brood over the other kids' reactions to the party invitations, because for the first time in weeks her whole family was gathered at the dinner table, and, as often happened, nobody was paying any attention to her. The talk was flying fast and furious. As usual, the conversation was dominated by Karen, who was bubbling on about her reactions to the college campuses she'd just visited.

"All the schools had official student guides to show the prospective students around," she explained. "The one at Brandham was a really adorable freshman guy from Chicago named Ernie Wallace. The two of us really hit it off. He laughed at every single thing I said."

Lexie thought of Shirley Spitzer, laughing whenever Kippy Meyer teased her at school. She'd said she did it because it was better than going around crying all the time. Lexie wondered if Ernie Wallace had actually been silently crying inside while he was giving Karen her campus tour.

"And you should have seen the library at Brandham!" Karen continued. "It's massive. And well-organized, too. Ernie was just going to give me a quick tour of the place, but I made him take me all over the building so I could check out how the stacks were arranged. They have an impressive selection of books, but if I end up going to school there, I do have a few suggestions to make about their cataloguing system."

Lexie felt a sudden surge of sympathy for Ernie Wallace, and decided she was definitely on the mark about the silent crying. Ever since Karen had started working part-time at the high school library, she'd become an enthusiastic fanatic about library science. She was already planning to go on to library school the instant she graduated from college.

"And do you know what else? The whole campus is a registered arboretum! They have little name plates on all the trees giving both the scientific and the common names!"

Mrs. Nielsen frowned at Mr. Nielsen and cleared her throat, but Karen was so excited she didn't notice. "It would be an educational experience just strolling along the walk to the cafeteria for breakfast!" she chirped. "You could learn a new tree every day! And just think of the . . ."

"Karen," Mrs. Nielsen interrupted gently. "I thought you liked all the schools you visited. But all we're hearing about tonight is Brandham."

"That's because it was absolutely the best, Mom. I'll just die if I don't get to go there!"

Mr. and Mrs. Nielsen exchanged another look, and all at once the family's cheery mood became tense. Even Daniel, who was usually oblivious to the atmosphere at the dinner table, sensed the change and momentarily stopped chewing his mouthful of marinated cabbage.

"I thought we agreed you wouldn't get your heart set on one place, honey," Mr. Nielsen said carefully. "Until we'd had a chance to work out the finances."

"I know we said that," Karen said. "But I didn't think you'd let me go visit a college you knew we wouldn't be able to afford. Besides, I *have* applied for a scholarship there. If I qualify for that, there won't be problem, will there?"

Mr. and Mrs. Nielsen looked at each other one last time. "We'll see," they both said at once.

Karen frowned and looked as if she'd like to say something else, but instead she picked up her fork and concentrated on her plateful of Thai food. Like all the children in the Nielsen family, she knew exactly what "we'll see" meant. It was her parents' code phrase for, "We'll make up our minds about this later when you're out of the room," and there was no point in arguing with it. In spite of their mother's commitment to family problem-solving procedures, a remarkable number of Nielsen family discussions ended with the phrase, "We'll see."

There were a few minutes of uncomfortable silence during which Lexie reflected on the fact that, contrary to what she'd thought, it seemed as if even when you were almost eighteen years old, you still couldn't make all your own decisions about everything. Then Mr. Nielsen introduced a new subject. "I heard a great shaggy dog story from Omar Schwartz at the office today. It seems there was once a group of men who were planning a fishing trip . . ."

With one voice, everyone at the table groaned. "It's one thing to put up with you and Lexie telling stupid riddles night after night, Daddy," Faith complained. "But do we have to sit through another one of Mr. Schwartz's shaggy dog stories? They don't even make any sense!"

In her heart, Lexie agreed with Faith about the shaggy dog stories, but she resented the remark about the stupid riddles, so she decided to stick up for her father. "No interrupting at the table, Faith," she said. "The rest of us are dying to hear Daddy's story."

Mr. Nielsen glanced at Karen, Daniel, and Mrs. Nielsen, who were all carefully studying the floral pattern on their china dinner plates. When no one said anything, he continued with his story. "It seems there was once a group of men who were planning a fishing trip," he repeated. "The three of them, Fred, Al, and Pete, had all been fishing together once before and they'd had a great time, except for one thing. They couldn't stand each other's cooking, and they'd gotten into some terrible fights about it.

"So this time, they decided to make a plan to avoid the fighting. They all agreed that the first person to complain about someone else's cooking would have to do all the cooking for the rest of the trip.

"The first day of the trip went fine except that the men didn't catch any fish, and all they had to cook for dinner was potatoes. It was Fred's turn to cook, and he made a fire, filled up a bucket with water and put the potatoes on to boil. After about half an hour, he took them off the fire and set the bucket down to cool. But, when he turned and walked away from the bucket, he knocked the salt off the top of the cooler, and the entire container spilled into the bucket! Neither Al nor Pete saw what had happened.

"Well, by this time, Al was nearly starving. He just couldn't wait to eat, so he picked up his fork, stabbed a potato, and bit into it. It was so salty, he nearly choked!

" *'That's the saltiest durn potato I ever ate!'* he screamed. Then, quick as a flash, he remembered the agreement about the cooking, and he said, 'But that's the way I like it!' "

The entire family stared at Mr. Nielsen in absolute silence, waiting for him to tell the end of the joke. When it finally dawned on them that this *was* the end of the joke, they all rolled their eyes at each other and groaned again.

Lexie was the only one who wasn't willing to give up. "That's *it,* Daddy?" she asked in amazement.

"That's it, kiddo."

"But what's the point?"

"I guess there isn't really a point." Mr. Nielsen picked up his fork and speared something pale and slippery. Lexie shuddered and looked away. "I still don't get it," she said.

"Well, there's really nothing to get, Lex," her father said as he popped the mystery food into his mouth. "That's what makes the story funny."

Daniel snorted, and Mr. Nielsen looked at him in disappointment. "In my opinion," Mrs. Nielsen said from her end of the table, "Omar Schwartz has outdone himself this time. He's sunk to a new low in humor."

"If you could call it humor," Lexie muttered. She picked up her sandwich and gave a little shrug. She had a lot of nerve, she realized, worrying about the kids at school thinking Shirley Spitzer was weird. What would the kids think if they heard her own father's dinnertime conversation for even one single night? Without a doubt, they'd conclude that the Nielsen house was the weirdest place in the whole wide world!

EIGHT

The next day at school Lexie found herself scanning the faces of her friends and classmates, trying to detect some kind of response to the birthday party invitation. Even though she realized the invitation had been sent out only the night before, and nobody could possibly have received one yet, she still had the paranoid feeling that all the kids already knew about it somehow and were going around whispering about it behind her back.

But right after school Gretchen Dietz came up to Lexie and acted perfectly normal. "Do you want to come over to my house again today?" she asked. "You could call your mom from there and see if it's okay."

Lexie thought guiltily of the thick pile of math homework she'd stuffed in her backpack, and she almost started to say no. But when she remembered how much fun she'd had the last time she'd gone to Gretchen's, she changed her mind. Math could always wait. "Sure!" she told Gretchen. "But I can't stay too late."

The two girls had just started out the classroom door when Suzy Frankowski and Cheryl Ingebrettson called to Lexie. "Hey, Lex!" Suzy said. "We're going to hang out at the park again this afternoon. Do you want to come?"

Lexie glanced at Gretchen. "Well," she began hesitantly, "I'm supposed to be going over to Gretchen's . . ."

"Gretchen can come, too," Cheryl said. "If you want to, that is, Gretchen."

"My mom gets pretty upset if I don't come home right after school," Gretchen said. "But how about this for a plan? We all go to my house, check in with my mom, pick up a snack, and *then* go to the park?"

"Good idea," Suzy said.

"*Great* idea," Lexie said happily, thinking of Mrs. Dietz's homemade chewy chocolate chip cookies. "Particularly the snack part."

The four of them trooped down the hallway and out onto the school grounds. Just outside the main door, they heard the shrill sound of Shirley Spitzer's hysterical giggle. Lexie looked over her shoulder and saw Shirley standing with her back pressed against the red brick wall of the school building. Kippy Meyer and Stevie Crawford were facing her. Kippy was busily making offensive blatting noises by putting his hands in his armpits and flapping his elbow up and down like a chicken wing.

The day before yesterday, Lexie would have laughed or made a disgusted face and kept right on walking along with her friends, and that's exactly what she *tried* to do today. It wasn't her business, she told herself. If she'd gone out a different door, she wouldn't even have known about Shirley and those boys.

But her feet didn't agree with her. All at once, they seemed to develop two little minds of their own. They forced her to slow down and stop only a few yards away from the school.

Lexie hesitated and chewed on her lip. "Wait a minute, guys," she said to her three friends. She turned around and walked back toward the building. "Hey, Shirley!" she called. "We're all going over to Gretchen's and then to the park. Do you want to come?"

Kippy stopped flapping his elbow and took his hand out from under his shirt. He and Stevie turned around to gape at Lexie. "Let me compliment you guys on your latest revolting achievement," she told them. "If there's a *Guinness Book of Grossness,* you two are sure to be in it."

Kippy and Stevie looked at each other and sniggered. Without saying anything, they drifted away from Shirley and Lexie and ran off around the corner to join a gang of boys playing Frisbee on the soccer field.

Lexie heard Gretchen, Cheryl, and Suzy come up behind her. She cleared her throat, swallowed hard, and quietly repeated her invitation to Shirley. "Do you want to come with us?"

Shirley stared at the three girls, and her eyes narrowed behind her thick glasses, as if she suspected a trick. Then Gretchen spoke up. "Why don't you come, Shirley? My mom won't care. She doesn't even know I'm bringing *anybody* home with me this afternoon, so one more person won't make a difference!"

At that moment, Lexie had to fight back an urge to fling her arms around Gretchen's neck and give her a big, sloppy kiss. What a terrific, fantastic person Gretchen was turning out to be. Suzy and Cheryl were old friends, and Lexie had been almost positive she could count on them to back her up no matter what she did. But she hadn't been at all sure how Gretchen would react, especially since Lexie was inviting Shirley to *Gretchen's* house!

The suspicious look slowly disappeared from Shirley's face. "Thanks for asking me," she said politely. "But

I can't come because my mom's picking me up to take me to the dentist."

"Ugh," Gretchen said. "Poor you. But maybe you can come to my house another time."

"Right," Lexie said. "We'll see you tomorrow, Shirley."

Shirley said good-bye, and Lexie and the other girls left the school grounds and headed toward Gretchen's house. As they walked along, Lexie sensed Suzy and Cheryl's curious sideways glances. They didn't want to say anything out loud in front of Gretchen, whom they didn't know very well, but Lexie knew exacty what they were wondering about. They were silently asking when and why Lexie Nielsen had suddenly become such good friends with strange Shirley Spitzer.

Lexie realized that this was the right time to tell the kids about the shared birthday party. She opened her mouth to do it. "Say, Gretchen," she said, "uh . . . umm . . . does your mom do that workout tape in front of the VCR every single day?"

"Sometimes she goes to an exercise class," Gretchen said. "In the mornings when I'm at school."

"My parents just got one of those big exercise bikes," Suzy said. "My dad put it in front of the TV right in the middle of the living room, and when he rides on it, he sweats like an absolute pig! I mean, there are sweat drops flying all over the room!"

The other girls giggled, and the subject of Shirley

Spitzer and the birthday party was temporarily banished from Lexie's mind. When they reached Lake Boulevard, she watched Cheryl's and Suzy's faces to see their reactions to the enormous size of Gretchen's house. As they went up the front walk to the Dietzes' home, both her friends' mouths dropped open in surprise.

Mrs. Dietz was waiting for Gretchen in the great room. Today instead of exercise clothes, she was wearing tailored black slacks and a black and white checkered blazer with big shoulders. Her hair was fluffed out in a circle of light, fluffy blonde curls. She had on another pair of dangling earrings, and her heart-shaped face was carefully made up. Lexie thought she looked more like a model than ever, and she could tell Cheryl and Suzy agreed with her. Ever since they'd first caught sight of Mrs. Dietz, their eyes had become enormous.

Mrs. Dietz's reaction to them wasn't quite so flattering. "Gretchen!" she said in dismay. "You haven't brought all these girls home *today!* Don't you remember I told you you're having a baby-sitter? Daddy's picking me up so we can go meet with the lawyer about Aunt Catherine's estate."

Gretchen looked embarrassed. "I told you I don't need a baby-sitter for just a couple of hours in the afternoon, Mom. But anyway, all we want to do is pack up a snack and go to the park for a while. So we wouldn't be here to bother Mrs. Swanson."

"Well," Mrs. Dietz said, "I'm not entirely comfortable with the arrangement, but since we won't be gone long, I suppose it's all right. But I'll have to double-check with Mrs. Swanson. And all you girls have to call your parents and let them know you're here under the supervision of a baby-sitter, in case of an emergency."

Lexie was sure neither of her parents would even be home yet and that even if they were, they wouldn't care who was supervising her. Nonetheless she and Suzy and Cheryl all dutifully promised to call home. Mrs. Dietz smiled. "Well, now that that's settled, I can remember my manners and say hello and welcome. I know Lexie, but I don't believe I've met the rest of you."

Gretchen introduced Cheryl and Suzy, and then Mrs. Dietz told them there were freshly baked oatmeal raisin cookies on the kitchen table. On the way out of the great room, Suzy whispered, "Say, Gretchen, where's the bathroom around here?"

"I have to go, too!" Lexie said.

"Me, too!" Cheryl giggled.

"Well, now that you've given me the idea, so do I!" Gretchen laughed. "Here's the plan. Suzy, you can use the little bathroom off the kitchen. Cheryl, you can use the one in the guest room, right down that hall. Lexie, you and I will have to go upstairs. Come on before it's too late!"

She took Lexie's hand and pulled her up a wide, white-carpeted staircase in the front hallway. When they were upstairs, she stopped at the first door she came to. "I'm desperate so I'll go in here," she said. "You go down the hall and use the one in my parents' bedroom. It's the last door on the left!"

Lexie walked down the hall, turned left, and stepped into the biggest bedroom she'd ever seen in her life. The powder-blue and white bed was big, too, and Lexie had to resist an impulse to go lie down on it to see if it felt as good as it looked. She gaped at the matching curtains and wall mirrors until she remembered why she was there and started looking around for a bathroom.

She reached out to turn the knob of a blue and white painted door that looked as if it had to be the right one. But when she stepped through the doorway, she found herself inside a huge walk-in closet instead of a bathroom. One wall was filled with hanging clothes and shoe racks. Along the other wall stood a dressing table and mirror. The table was covered with face creams, hand lotions, perfume bottles, hair sprays, lipsticks, blushes, eye shadows, eyebrow pencils, eyeliners, and assorted other cosmetics Lexie didn't even recognize.

She had never seen so much makeup in her life. Without really thinking about what she was doing, she walked forward and sat down on the small white leather stool in front of the table. She was studying a tray full of different shades of pale brown eye shadow when Mrs. Dietz walked into the closet. "Now where did I put that black purse . . . ? Lexie! You surprised me!"

Lexie's cheeks flushed, and she looked up with a

guilty start. "Uh . . . hi!" she said, jumping to her feet. "I was trying to find the bathroom, and I came in here by mistake and . . . well, I started looking at the makeup and . . ."

"Don't worry about it," Mrs. Dietz said. "This house is such a big barn people are always getting lost in it. When we first moved in, we couldn't even find each other!" She looked on a shelf and found the purse she wanted. "Come on, Lexie. I'll show you the door to the bathroom."

"Thanks," Lexie said, following her toward the door. She glanced back at the dressing table. "You sure have a lot of makeup!"

"Believe me, Lexie, I use it *all*. Old ladies like me need every bit of help we can get!"

Lexie stared at Mrs. Dietz's pretty face in disbelief. "You want to know something incredible?" she said after a few seconds. "My mom hardly uses any makeup at all—even when she goes out to a party!"

"Your mom?" Gretchen's mother looked into a wall mirror and fluffed out a curl over her forehead. "Your mom is Barbara Nielsen, right?"

"Right. You said you met her at a PTA meeting once."

"I certainly did. And I can tell you right now, if I looked like she does, I wouldn't wear much makeup either. You wouldn't want to cover up that Scandinavian bone structure and coloring with makeup! Believe me, you just couldn't get that kind of classic look out of a bottle." She opened another door next to the closet. "The bathroom's right in here, Lexie. I have to run now. I think I just heard my husband pull in the drive. Can you find your way downstairs by yourself?"

Lexie mumbled something, and Gretchen's mother smiled, and said good-bye. After Mrs. Dietz had left, Lexie barely noticed she was alone again. She stood stock-still with shock, frozen in the middle of the blue and white bedroom. Her mind simply couldn't accept what she'd just heard. A glamorous, beautiful, perfectly groomed person like Mrs. Dietz thought Lexie's preoccupied, hurried, wispy-haired mom had a "classic look." It had never occurred to Lexie that someone might think of *her* mother in that way!

Of course it was possible Mrs. Dietz hadn't really meant what she'd said, Lexie thought. Maybe she was just trying to be nice. But what if she *had* meant it? What if Mom actually *was* pretty? Did it really mean anything?

She knew exactly what her mother would say about it, of course. She'd say it didn't make the slightest bit of difference what Mrs. Dietz thought of her looks. But for some reason, to Lexie it did mean something—even though she could never in a million years have explained exactly what it was.

NINE

The next night after dinner the kids from school started calling up to respond to the birthday party invitation. To Lexie's surprise, most of them didn't even say anything about the party's being given by two people, except for Kippy Meyer, who asked if he really had to bring two presents. The rest of the people who called wanted to know exactly what B.Y.O.A. meant.

"Just what it says," Lexie explained. "It means 'bring your own activity.' "

"But what kind of activity are we supposed to bring?" Suzy Frankowski asked.

"You don't really have to bring anything. You just have to be responsible for some kind of activity that would be fun at a birthday party. But try to think of something wild and original."

"That's easy for you to say!" Suzy said. "You don't have to think of anything."

"Yes, I do. Shirley and I are each planning one activity, just like everybody else."

Suzy hesitated. Then she asked, "Is your mom making you have this party with Shirley?"

"Well, you know how bossy my mom is . . . ," Lexie began automatically. Then she stopped herself, remembering her mother's words about taking the easy way out. She cleared her throat and started over again. "To tell you the truth, the whole thing was my idea. I told everybody I was going to come up with a really different birthday idea this year, and, well . . . this is it!"

"It sure is," Suzy said dryly. "It's a little *too* different, if you ask me! I just know I won't be able to think of anything good to do."

"Sure you will," Lexie said. "Are you watching the Twins game tonight? It starts in five minutes."

"I'll go turn it on. See you tomorrow!"

Lexie hung up and went to turn on the TV. When the phone rang a few seconds later, she assumed it was for her again and started back into the kitchen to answer it. Karen, who'd just finished washing the pots and pans, beat her to it. "Hello?" she said. "Yes. Yes. Oh, *yes!* He's here. Just a minute, I'll call him."

She put her hand over the mouthpiece. "Daddy. *Dadeeee!*" Mr. Nielsen trudged up the stairs from the basement and reached for the telephone. "It's Lexie's teacher, Mr. Snyder," Karen continued in a dramatic stage whisper. "He wants to talk to either you or Mom, but she's out, so I called you. He does *not* sound happy. Lexie must be having some kind of problem in school."

Lexie shot Karen a dark look and started to back out the door, but her father motioned for her to stay. To her intense disgust, Lexie noticed her sister start ostentatiously puttering around the kitchen, even though she'd finished loading the dishwasher several minutes ago. She was blatantly eavesdropping on the telephone conversation. To make matters worse, she probably didn't even think there was anything wrong with doing it. As the oldest sibling in the family, Karen saw herself in the role of parents' aide, freely dishing out valuable advice to their mother and father about how they should deal with their other children.

"Uh-huh," Mr. Nielsen was saying. "You don't say. Well, we didn't know a thing about that. Of course. We'll see that she does. Thank you for your trouble."

Lexie's father put down the phone and faced Lexie with a stern expression. "Lexie, I have a good idea you know exactly what that call was about. Mr. Snyder says you haven't turned in a single piece of your math homework for two weeks."

As if she'd just been slapped across the face, Karen gasped in shock and pain. "Lexie!" she exclaimed in a hushed voice. "Really! What are we going to do with you?"

Lexie scowled ferociously, and Mr. Nielsen gave Karen an irritated look. "Karen," he said, "don't you have something else to do?"

"Well, of course I do!" Karen said indignantly. "I actually *do* my homework!" She stomped out of the room, and Lexie's scowl grew even darker.

"Why does she always have to butt in like that?" she began. "I mean, just exactly who does she think she . . . ?"

"Lexie! Stop trying to change the subject. You are going to march into the living room right now, get out every piece of that math homework, sit down at the desk, and do it!"

"But, Daddy," Lexie whined. "I hate it! It's so boring."

"Well, I'm sorry you feel that way, Lexie. But if you want to have that birthday party next week, you'll finish that homework tonight."

Lexie blinked. She couldn't believe her father was actually threatening to call off her birthday party. All at once, she felt very sorry for herself. "I don't like the math, Daddy," she said in a trembling voice. "It's hard."

"Life is hard, Lexie. And sometimes we have to do things we don't want to do. Most people don't like hard work, but we have to do it anyway." He followed her into the living room and frowned as he watched her take her math book and a crumpled pile of math work sheets from her backpack. "Do you know what you're supposed to do?" he asked. "Can you figure out the problems?"

"I guess so," Lexie sighed.

"I'll go back down to the basement then, kiddo. Call me if you need help."

"Okay, Daddy." Fat chance, Lexie told herself. The last time she'd asked her father to help her with math, he'd ended up making her more confused than she'd been in the first place! He was good with things like words and people, and he knew a lot about birds and flowers and nature, but when it came to numbers, he was even worse than Lexie.

Lexie smoothed out her first work sheet and heaved another sigh as she remembered why she'd stopped doing her math homework in the first place. It wasn't just that it was boring and stupid. She didn't have the slightest idea how to do it!

When Daniel walked through the door a half hour later, she had her face buried in her arms and was quietly crying onto the desk blotter. "Man, am I hungry!" he said as he sauntered in surrounded by his usual McDonald's aroma. "Hi, Lex. . . . say, what's the matter with you?"

Lexie wiped her face with her hand and gestured toward the pile of work sheets on the desk. "Math," she said tearfully. "I hate it. *And* I can't do it. But Daddy says if I don't, I can't have my birthday party!"

"Whoa!" Daniel exclaimed. "This is serious. But have no fear! Didn't you know your brother is actually SuperMath in disguise?"

"No." Lexie giggled through her tears. "Your secret identity must be very effective." Actually the truth was that she did know Daniel was good at math. He was good at everything. Not only was he the star of every single sports team at the high school, he also got all A's in every single subject. And they were all Advanced Placement classes!

"What kind of math are you doing?"

Lexie glanced down at the top work sheet. "I think it must be fractions," she said doubtfully.

"Fractions! SuperMath eats them for breakfast!" Daniel dropped his bookbag onto the floor. "Which reminds me that I'm starving. Just let me go microwave myself this frozen pizza I picked up at the convenience store, and I'll be back in a minute."

"How can you be hungry?" Lexie called after him. "After wallowing in all those french fries at McDonalds?"

"French fries!" Daniel repeated in disgust. "I hope I never see another one. Believe me, after spending all that time dishing them out to customers, I'd rather eat an extra-large box of deep fat-fried worms than eat a single french fry!"

He went into the kitchen, where Lexie heard him clattering around for a few minutes. When he returned to the living room, he was balancing an extra-large Mama DeGrassi's pizza on a small plate. Now the smell of burgers and fries combined with the smell of tomato sauce, pepperoni, and melted cheese. Lexie's mouth started to water.

"So what kind of fraction problems are we talking about here?" Daniel asked, taking a bite out of his pizza and pulling up another chair.

Lexie blinked at him. She couldn't believe this was actually happening. Usually, Daniel didn't pay the slightest bit of attention to her, except to tell her to pass the taco sauce or get off the phone or stop taking his cassettes without asking. Being ignored by Daniel was a fact of Lexie's life, and she was used to it. But now, out of the blue, he was acting like some kind of saintly big brother out of a TV show! What could have come over him?

"Lexie! Do you want me to help you or not? Because if you don't, I have plenty of other things I could be doing!"

That sounded more like the Daniel she knew. Lexie

knew she'd better hurry up and make the most of what remained of her brother's unusually helpful good mood. "I think we're supposed to multiply the fractions," she said quickly. "Or maybe divide them."

Daniel leaned over to look at the work sheet himself. "You're supposed to multiply them," he said through a second mouthful of pizza. "Here. It says one-half times one-half. That's easy. Go ahead and do that one."

"Let's see. Ummm. I guess one-half times one-half ought to come out to . . . about one?"

Daniel stared at her and stopped chewing. "About one?" he repeated.

"Well, exactly one, then."

"Come on, Lexie. You know better than that! Half of a half can't be *one!*"

Lexie put her face back down on the desk and started to cry again. "I can't doooo it!" she wailed. "When you multiply something it's supposed to get bigger. But it never works with fractions. I hate this!"

"Okay, okay, don't get excited, I have an idea." Daniel put his pizza plate on the floor, got up, and ran out of the living room. He came back carrying a big black pair of kitchen shears. "Let's take a look at Mr. Pizza here," he said, picking up his plate again. "Now first we'll take half of it, like this." He cut into the pizza, sloppily hacking it into two basically equal parts. "Now, according to you, if we multiply something it should get bigger, and that's absolutely true with whole numbers. But when you multiply something by a fraction, it should get smaller, like this." Using the sauce-covered shears again, he divided one half of the pizza into two equal parts. "One-half times one-half is . . . ?"

"I can't tell because you took two big bites out of that part."

"Lexie, stop being so dense! Forget the bites! Pretend this is a brand-new pizza."

"Okay. Um, so . . . it looks like . . . well, I mean, isn't that little part one-fourth?" Lexie asked hesitantly.

"Right!" Daniel said. He popped the one-fourth into his mouth. "I can't believe you don't know this. Your teacher really should have explained it to you."

"He probably did," Lexie said. "I just wasn't listening."

"Well, you should have been! How do you expect to understand this stuff if you don't listen to your teacher?"

Lexie made a face at him. "You sound *exactly* like Karen, Daniel," she said.

"You don't have to get nasty, Lexie!" He chewed on a piece of pepperoni and pointed to the work sheet. "Read me the next problem."

Lexie read him the next problem, which the two of them solved together. Amazingly, after that she was able to do the rest of the multiplication problems by herself, but she needed Daniel's advice again when she started a new page. With her brother's help, she'd soon worked her way through the entire pile of work sheets. When she triumphantly finished the last problem on the last page, she looked up to see Daniel staring at his watch and yawning.

"It's been fun, Lex," he said, getting to his feet. "But I have to go to bed now. I'm getting up at five to go running on the track up at school tomorrow morning."

"But we still haven't done the 'Think and Learn' problems in the book!" Lexie cried in alarm.

"Well, *we* aren't going to do them tonight!" He patted her on top of the head. "You'll just have to think and learn by yourself."

Lexie jumped up from her chair and yanked on Daniel's arm. "Come on, Daniel. You have to help me. Please!"

Daniel pried her fingers off his arm. "Knock it off, Lexie!" he said sharply. "Stop being such a little pest."

He walked out of the room, and Lexie looked after him and sighed. Oh, well, she told herself. Things with her brother were back to normal again. It had been too good to last, anyway.

She picked up the pile of work sheets and put them back into her backpack. Then she put her math textbook into the backpack as well. Maybe she'd get up early tomorrow and do the "Think and Learn" problems, she told herself. Or better yet, maybe she wouldn't do them at all, and Mr. Snyder would forget all about them. And even if he didn't forget, maybe he'd get so excited when he saw the big pile of completed work sheets, he'd forgive her for not doing the other work right away. Maybe he'd say she made such a good effort, he didn't care if she ever did the "Think and Learn" problems.

She put down the backpack and noticed Daniel's dirty pizza plate sitting in the middle of the floor. Even though she knew it wasn't her responsibility, she decided to clean it up for him.

After all, she thought as she carried the plate into the kitchen, even though Daniel had called her a pest, he had helped her out a lot. He'd gotten her out of trouble with Mr. Snyder and with her father. And he'd also saved her from having her birthday party canceled!

TEN

The week before the birthday party went very slowly, particularly during school hours. Contrary to what she'd hoped, Mr. Snyder did notice Lexie had neglected to do any of the "Think and Learn" problems from the textbook, and he made her stay inside every day during recess to work on them. Even though she was dying to go outside, Lexie found the problems so boring and silly—what difference did it make that Dan was older than Lynn who was older than Jane who was younger than Tom?—that it took her forever to finish them. By the time she'd complete just one problem, the other kids would already be coming back into the classroom, ready to begin the afternoon's work.

Lexie could hardly wait to get home each day after school. The afternoon and evening hours went slowly, too, but they were more fun. Lexie spent her time planning and replanning her activity for the party, as well as talking to her friends about the activities they were planning. By Tuesday, Lexie had spoken to every single girl in her class besides Shirley, but she still didn't have the slightest idea what the boys were planning to do. As the week went on, she grew more and more anxious. What if nobody liked anyone else's activities? What if some of the boys tried to do something idiotic? She could just imagine the kind of activity Kippy Meyer might plan. It would undoubtedly be something repulsive—like seeing who could stuff the biggest bug up somebody else's nose.

By Friday afternoon, Lexie was in an emotional state, positive the party was going to be a total flop. She brooded about new and more horrible disastrous possibilities. Nobody would come. Everybody would come, but they wouldn't have any fun, and they'd all walk out. Everybody would come, but they'd all make fun of Shirley, and Lexie would have to stick up for her, and then they'd all make fun of Lexie. The entire party would be a living nightmare from beginning to end, and it would all be Lexie Nielsen's fault.

As she grew more and more agitated, Lexie realized she was on the verge of making herself sick to her stomach. She tried to calm herself down by thinking of ways to make the party succeed. The most important thing, she decided, was to be sure there was a lot of good food around to keep the kids happy and distracted. Shirley's parents were bringing ice cream and party favors, but the Nielsens were responsible for the cake and other snacks. After school on Friday, Lexie nagged Karen into giving her a ride to the supermarket to buy gum, M&M's, peanuts, cheese curls, and mini-pizzas. But by 8:00 Friday evening, there was still no sign of the cake. Lexie decided to go in search of her mother to find out when she was planning to make it.

She found both her parents downstairs in the basement, huddled in front of the computer. Several columns of numbers appeared on the screen, and she could hear her father muttering words like, "budget," "finances," and "income." Her mother said, "quality education" once or twice, and Lexie realized her parents were trying to figure out if they could afford to send Karen to Brandham next year.

She waited for the two of them to stop talking for a minute so she could ask about the cake. "Mom," she said, "when are we going to . . . ?"

"Lexie, can it wait?" her father said without turning around. "We're right in the middle of something here."

"But this is important, Daddy! I have to talk to Mom."

Mrs. Nielsen swiveled around to look at her, and Lexie noticed two little worry lines furrowed between her mother's pale blue eyes. "Mom, when are we going to make my birthday cake?"

Her mother turned back toward the computer. "I don't think we're going to have time to make one this year, Lex," she said. "I thought I'd stop off at Waldman's on my way home tomorrow morning and pick one up there."

"You're getting my birthday cake from a supermarket?" Lexie asked indignantly.

"Well, yes, but they have that nice new bakery section where they bake everything on the premises."

"But you always make my cake!"

Mrs. Nielsen turned around again. "Well, I know I usually have made your cake in the past, Lexie . . ."

"Not usually. *Always!*"

"All right, always. But this year I have to go somewhere in the morning, so I thought . . ."

"You're going somewhere on the very morning of my birthday party? Who's going to help me get ready?"

"Lexie, could you please lower your voice just a little?" Mr. Nielsen put in. "When you hit those high registers, my ears start to vibrate, and it's very painful."

"Yes, I am going somewhere, Lexie," Mrs. Nielsen said. "Penelope Dove's going to be on a radio talk show, and they want me to be at the station with her to help her out with information for the questions she'll be asked. You know the school board election is next week, and everything we do right now is important."

All of a sudden, Lexie snapped. Taking her parents completely by surprise, she burst into wild, hysterical tears and started screaming at the top of her lungs. "Everything and everybody are more important to you than my birthday party!" she shouted. "Shirley Spitzer and Penelope Dove and all your meetings and your classes at the U and everything else in the whole world are all more important than me and my feelings!"

Both her parents were staring at her now. The numbers on the computer screen were completely forgotten. "Lexie," her father said in a warning voice. "Hold on for just a minute here, young lady."

But Lexie was too overwrought to listen to him. "You say you're supporting Penelope Dove because she cares about all the children. Well, maybe she does. But *you* don't, Mom! You don't even care about your own children! You don't buy us any food, and you never cook us anything. You're never even here anymore! You were already twice as busy as any normal mother before, but did that stop you? No! You had to go get involved in the school board election! Well, go ahead and *go* to the stupid radio station tomorrow. Stay all day if you want! See if *I* care!"

She whirled around, turning her back on her parents'

shocked faces. Then, almost blinded by her tears, she ran up the two flights of stairs to her room, slammed her door, threw herself facedown on the bed, and sobbed into her pillow. She was still crying an hour later when Faith came home from baby-sitting for the Larsens and started getting ready for bed.

"What's your problem now, floodface?"

Lexie flipped over onto her back and sat up. "Didn't Mom and Daddy tell you about it?" she asked through her sniffles. "Aren't they going to come up here and reason with me or anything?"

"They were having a discussion in front of the computer when I came in, and they didn't tell me anything about anything," Faith said, sitting down on the edge of her bed. She pulled off one of her shoes and started rubbing her toes. "That little brat Donny Larsen stomped my foot when I tried to get him into bed," she complained. "So anyway, what happened here?"

"I had a big fight with Mom," Lexie said, wiping her eyes with her fingers. "I mean, I really screamed at her."

"What about?"

"Well, she said she was going to get my birthday cake at Waldman's tomorrow!"

"So?"

"So that means she's not making it this year!"

"So that's what you screamed at her about? What's the big deal about that? Those cakes from Waldman's are really good! I had a piece of chocolate fudge cake from there at Becky Brady's party last month, and it was fantastic!" Faith's face took on a dreamy expression. In Nielsen family folklore, she was famous for having the biggest sweet tooth.

Lexie sighed in exasperation. "It's not just the cake, Faith! It's everything lately. Mom's always so busy, and she's never here, and she never even goes to the store . . . and just everything! She cares about everybody but us. Take my party, for instance. It's a perfect example of what I'm talking about. Mom knew I really wanted to have a special little party with just a few kids. But did she let me? No! The minute she heard about poor Shirley Spitzer, she got all worried about her and decided Shirley's problems were more important than mine. Mom puts everybody else before her own family! She doesn't even care about us anymore!"

Faith stopped in the middle of taking off her other shoe. "You actually *said* that to Mom?"

"A lot of it, yes."

"Wow." Faith finished taking off her shoe. "Wow."

Lexie scowled. "What's that supposed to mean?"

"Well, I don't know exactly. I guess I just can't believe you had the nerve to come right out and say that stuff to Mom. I mean, I know she's been super-busy lately, and she can be a real pain in the neck about how we're all responsible for the whole world, blah, blah, blah, but *still* . . ."

"*Still,* what?"

"Well, it sounds like you were pretty mean to her!"

"You'd be mean, too, if your birthday party was getting all messed up!"

Faith got up and started pacing the floor in her bare feet. "Why are you so obsessed with your moronic birthday party, Lexie?" she asked. "For Pete's sake, you're going to be ten years old tomorrow! You don't really need your mommy to help you put peanuts into the snack cups anymore, do you? And besides, I think it's sort of exciting Mom's going to help Penelope Dove at the radio station. It must mean old Penelope thinks Mom is pretty smart. But do you care about that? No! You're such a spoiled baby, all you care about is getting your little birthday balloons blown up!"

Lexie glared at her sister, desperately trying to come up with something nasty to say back to her. But she couldn't think of a thing, and slowly, she felt her hot, self-righteous anger begin to cool. Could Faith possibly be right? Lexie asked herself in dismay. Was she acting like a spoiled baby, thinking only about herself?

All at once inside her mind, Lexie heard the sound of her own hysterical voice, screaming all those horrible insults at her mother downstairs in the basement. She moaned, flipped back over onto her face, and started quietly weeping into her pillow again.

ELEVEN

Long after Faith had fallen asleep and started to snore, Lexie continued fitfully tossing and turning in her hot, tangled sheets. Sometimes she cried, and sometimes she stared wide-eyed up at the floating shadows the moonlight created on the ceiling. Finally, when the gloved hands on her Bugs Bunny alarm clock pointed to one minute to midnight, she decided to get up and go for another drink of water. As she walked out of her bedroom, she heard noises coming from downstairs.

She crept along the hallway and listened outside Karen's and Daniel's bedroom doors. Like Faith, they were both sound asleep, snoring like a pair of lawnmowers. Lexie frowned. Who on earth could be walking around downstairs at this hour? she asked herself. Her exhausted old parents never stayed up until midnight!

She went on down the hall and stood at the top of the steps, listening hard. Finally, curiosity got the better of her. Trying not to think about the old sea captain, she tiptoed downstairs to the first floor.

She found her mother in the kitchen, scooping flour out of a canister and pouring it into a mixing bowl. Mrs. Nielsen didn't see her at first, and for a minute, Lexie stood quietly in the doorway. As she watched, she stared at her mother's face, trying to see some sign of the "classic look" Mrs. Dietz had mentioned the other day, but it was no use. To Lexie, her mother looked the way she always had. She was just plain old wispy-haired Mom, looking slightly more tired than usual.

A floorboard creaked under Lexie's feet, and Mrs. Nielsen glanced up and saw her. The two of them stared at each other for a long moment. Lexie was sure her mother was going to ask her what she was doing out of bed in the middle of the night, but instead Mrs. Nielsen just smiled at her. "Hi, honey," she said. "I'm making yellow cake with chocolate icing. Isn't that your favorite kind?"

Lexie ran into the room and threw her arms around her mother's waist. Mrs. Nielsen bent down and hugged her back. "I'm sorry I've been so busy lately, Lexie," she said. "And I'm sorry about the cake. I didn't realize a homemade cake was so important to you."

"I'm the one who's sorry, Mom!" Lexie burst out, starting to cry again. "I didn't mean a single thing I said before!"

Mrs. Nielsen shook her head. "I think you meant quite a bit of it, Lexie," she said. "I think it was a very healthy outburst on your part. You really vented some genuine pent-up emotion and preadolescent frustration and . . ."

"Mom," Lexie interrupted anxiously. "You're not trying to start a counseling session with me, are you?"

Her mother laughed. "No, I swear I'm not! I just meant that I'm not mad you yelled at me. I think you made some good points. In fact, based on what you said, tomorrow morning I'm going to call up Penelope and ask her to find somebody else to go to the radio station with her."

Lexie leaned back and stared up at her mother's flour-streaked face. "But, Mom! Don't you really want to go be on the show?"

"I guess part of me wants to go, but part of me wants to stay and help you get ready for your party."

"Well, it's okay with me if both parts of you go," Lexie said. "Since the kids are bringing their own activities, there really isn't that much to do before they get here anyway."

Mrs. Nielsen pushed a flyaway wisp of hair back into her bun. "Hmmm," she said thoughtfully. "We'll see." She gazed down at her daughter and gave her another hug. "Being a mom has its rewards, Lexie," she continued, "but it's not alway easy."

"Well, believe me, it's *never* easy being a kid!"

"I guess you're right about that. Do you want to help me finish making your cake?"

"Even though it's the middle of the night?"

"Even though it's the middle of the night!" Mrs. Nielsen handed her a bowl. "Come on, Lexie. I need you to taste this batter for me. I wasn't concentrating, and I think I may have put an extra cup of sugar in by mistake."

Lexie stuck her finger into the bowl and slurped up a big dollop of batter. Her eyes grew wide. "Mom," she said, "this is the sweetest batter I ever tasted . . . *but that's the way I like it!*"

The echo of Mr. Nielsen's terrible joke struck both Lexie and her mother as extremely funny, and the two of them doubled over in a fit of hysterical giggles. They were still giggling over an hour later when they took the cake out of the oven and told each other good night.

TWELVE

The day of Lexie and Shirley's birthday party was bright and warm. Even though she'd stayed up half the night, Lexie was too excited to feel tired the next morning. She became even more excited when she came downstairs for breakfast and found a gorilla waiting for her in the front hall.

Before Lexie could ask him what he was doing there, the gorilla started tap dancing and grunting out a song.

Happy birthday to my friend Lexie,
*Who's ten years old to*day!
I wish I could come to your party,
*But I'm stuck in Californ-i-*ay!
I miss you very much,
I wish I could be there soon!
But my mom says I have to stay here,
So I can't come home till June!

The gorilla stopped singing, got down on his knees, handed Lexie a big bouquet of balloons, and growled, "Happy birthday to Lexie from her best friend Debby in California."

"Thank you," Lexie said. She patted the gorilla on the top of his head. The fake fur on his mask felt like the bristles on an old paintbrush. "I'm sorry, but we're all out of bananas."

The gorilla grunted and headed for the door. When he was gone, Lexie asked if she could call Debby to thank her, but her father reminded her it was only 7:00 A.M. in California. Just then, the phone rang. Karen answered it in the kitchen.

"Lexie!" she called out. "It's for you."

Lexie went into the kitchen and reached for the phone. "It's one of your little boyfriends!" Karen said, without even bothering to cover the mouthpiece with her hand.

Lexie made a face at her and grabbed the phone. To

her surprise, Kippy Meyer was on the other end of the line.

"Is it okay if me and Stevie and the other boys come to the party about half an hour early?" he asked. "We have to set some stuff up in your backyard."

"Well, sure, I guess it's okay," Lexie said. "Come whenever you want." She hung up the phone and started rummaging around in the refrigerator, looking for something to eat for breakfast. Just then, her mother hurried into the kitchen.

"Happy birthday, ten-year-old!" she said, kissing Lexie on top of her head. "My youngest child has finally made it into double digits."

"Where are my presents?" Lexie asked.

"I told you, honey, we're saving family presents until dinner tonight. That way they don't get lost in the shuffle."

"I know, Mom! I was *joking*. You missed my singing gorilla."

"No, I didn't. I was watching from the top of the stairs, but I didn't want to come down in my bathrobe."

Lexie noticed that her mother was wearing a skirt and blouse, an outfit that for Mrs. Nielsen qualified as being dressed up. "Did you decide to go to the radio station, Mom?" she asked.

"I made a compromise with myself," her mother said, putting a piece of bread into the toaster. "I'll go down for part of the show, but I'll leave before the end."

"Okay," Lexie said. In her heart, she was sure her mother would never be able to get away before the end of the program, but it didn't really bother her very much. She was too excited to let much of anything bother her today.

She ate some frozen waffles drowned in maple syrup for breakfast, and then she and her mother started stringing crepe paper and banners around the house. When they finished decorating, they started opening bags of chips and cheese curls and emptying them into big plastic bowls. Before long, it was time for Mrs. Nielsen to leave, at which point Mr. Nielsen started helping out. He sat down in a chair in the living room and started blowing up balloons. Within a few minutes, he was light-headed and blue in the face.

By 12:00, all the preparations were over. At 12:30 the doorbell rang, and Faith let in Shirley and both her parents. Mr. and Mrs. Spitzer hurried into the kitchen to put away the ice cream.

Lexie said hi to Shirley and started to ask her what activity she'd brought, but before Shirley could say anything, the doorbell rang again. This time, Karen answered the door. "Lexie, there are ten boys standing out here!" she called.

"Send them around to the backyard, please!" Lexie yelled back. She turned to Shirley and whispered, "Let's sneak up on the roof and spy on what they're doing."

But no sooner had the two girls scrambled up to the rooftop than they saw Gretchen Dietz, Suzy Frankowski, and Cheryl Ingebrettson walking along the sidewalk below. They looked at each other, shrugged, and climbed back down to greet the rest of their guests.

By 1:00 on the dot, all 22 fourth-graders were gathered in the living room, waiting for the party to start. "Who wants to go first?" Lexie asked.

"I think I should," Gretchen said. "My activity needs some time to dry." She dumped out the contents of two big paper bags onto the floor. "It's T-shirt painting," she explained. "I have special little tubes of paint and a T-shirt for each kid."

Immediately, everybody scrambled to grab a shirt. Mr. Nielsen came into the room and saw the paint. "Outside!" he cried in alarm. "Take all that paint out into the front yard on the double."

The whole class trooped out onto the front lawn where they spent the next several minutes happily creating their own designer T-shirts. While they were painting, Mrs. Nielsen pulled up in the station wagon and jumped out of the car.

"Sorry I'm late, Lex!" she said breathlessly.

"No sweat, Mom," Lexie said, dropping a glob of fluorescent red paint onto her shirt. "We didn't even need you."

When all the T-shirts were finished and lying in the sun to dry, several of the girls asked to put on their activities. Soon the crowd was divided into smaller groups busily playing musical chairs and pin-the-tail-on-the-donkey. Cheryl and Suzy brought out some hysterically funny charades they'd written for everybody to act out for everybody else. Then Lauren Lindskog brought out a big easel and taught everybody how to play a guessing game called Pictionary.

The only activity that nobody liked was Brooke's. She wanted to play a game called "Identify that Quotation."

"I stand up in front of everybody," she explained, "and say a famous quote. Then you all have to guess who said it. Here's the first one. 'Give me liberty or give me death.' "

Nobody said a word until Kippy Meyer spoke up. "*I* have a famous quotation," he said, " 'This game stinks!' And guess who said it! Me!"

Brooke glared at him. "Well, if you don't like my activity, why don't you show us yours then, Kippy? I'm sure it's absolutely perfect!"

"I'm sure you're right!" he said. With a wave of his hand, he led a charge around the corner of the house to the backyard, where the boys had set up a variety of elaborate paraphernalia.

"Welcome to the Birthday Party Olympics!" Stevie Crawford cried. "We have an obstacle course, a raw egg toss, a three-legged race, a water balloon fight, and a teaspoon relay."

"And don't forget my activity!" Kippy said.

Stevie rolled his eyes. "Right. Kippy has a special activity at the end."

After that, the kids divided themselves into groups again, and rotated around the yard, participating in each event in the Birthday Party Olympics. Soon the remains of raw eggs and water balloons littered the grass, but the boys and girls were having so much fun they hardly noticed the mess.

At one point, halfway through the cardboard box tunnel on the obstacle course, Lexie bumped heads with Shirley. They stopped crawling, lay down flat on their stomachs, and grinned at each other.

"This party's going down in history," Lexie commented.

"You bet," Shirley agreed. "But I wonder what activity Kippy has up his sleeve."

Lexie grimaced. "I'm trying not to think about it," she said as she crawled away. "But I'm sure it will be gross."

A few minutes later, when she finished jumping through a hula hoop, she found out just how right she'd been. Kippy was waving his arms, calling everybody together, and telling them to sit down on the grass. "Come right over here!" he yelled. "It's time for the start of the Birthday Party Olympics Burping Contest."

Suzy let out a loud groan, and Brooke clucked her tongue. Several of the boys immediately started burping as loudly as they could. A few of them burped so much they sounded as if they were going to throw up. Even though Lexie had to admit the whole thing was pretty funny, she felt as if she were losing control of the party and wondered if she should go inside and call her parents. But just then, Shirley got to her feet.

Slowly, she stalked to the front of the group. For some reason, at that moment all the boys decided to stop burping. The group of kids became completely silent. Shirley climbed over Gretchen's legs and walked right up to Kippy Meyer. She kept going until she was only a few inches away from him. She took a big swallow of air. And then she burped in his face.

Shirley's burp was so loud and so resonant, it echoed throughout the backyard, ricocheting off the picket fence and bouncing back to be appreciated a second time. Kippy staggered backward, his mouth dropping open in astonishment. There was a moment of appreciative silence, during which Lexie stared at Shirley in surprise. She couldn't believe she was looking at the same person. What had happened to shy, insecure Shirley who thought she had to giggle every time somebody teased her? She was standing up there in front of all the other kids, *burping right in Kippy Meyer's face!*

All at once, Lexie felt as if she deserved to share in Shirley's triumph. She jumped to her feet and started clapping. "Bravo!" she screamed. "Encore!"

Soon all the kids, including the boys, were clapping,

pounding Shirley on the back and saying things like, "Way to go, Shirley! You really showed him! How'd you do that, anyway?" Even Kippy was clapping. He was looking at Shirley with new respect, as if he'd never really seen her before.

After the noise died down, Lexie remembered that she hadn't done her activity yet. She ran into the house and came back out with a huge garbage bag, out of which she dumped twenty rolls of toilet paper. "This may look like another gross activity," she said. "But it's not. It's a make-your-own-mummy game. Each person needs to find a partner. Then you use a roll or two of toilet paper to turn that person into a mummy. My dad's going to make a movie of the whole thing, and we'll make you copies of it for party favors."

The kids scurried to find partners. Lexie turned to find Shirley, but then saw that Shirley was already paired with Gretchen. To her disappointment, Lexie finally ended up with Brooke, but that turned out not to be so bad after all. In fact, there was something very satisfying about wrapping Brooke's head with toilet paper. Lexie wrapped Brooke up so securely that when she was finished, she was sure her mummy was the most authentic-looking of all.

Mr. Nielsen videotaped the mummification activity and declared it was time for refreshments. The whole group hastily peeled off their wrappings, filling seven garbage bags with the bulky loose toilet paper. They charged into the kitchen, where Shirley finally revealed her activity. "It's called make-your-own-sundae," she said, handing out red plastic spoons. She pointed to the table, which was covered with boxes of vanilla and chocolate chocolate chip ice cream and little bowls filled with strawberries, peanuts, candy, coconut, sprinkles, cookie crumbs, smashed Heath bars, chocolate chips, cherries, whipped cream, butterscotch, and hot fudge. "The person with the most artistic sundae takes home all the leftovers."

Everybody crowded around the table and busied themselves scooping out mounds of ice cream and decorating them with all the toppings. The room got so noisy, Mr. Nielsen finally had to bang on the countertop to get the group's attention. "Ahem!" he said. "I believe it's cake time."

Mrs. Nielsen and Mrs. Spitzer walked into the kitchen, carrying the large sheet cake Lexie and her mother had made the night before. Twenty candles glowed on top of the rich chocolate frosting. As everybody started singing "Happy Birthday," Lexie exchanged a look with her mother, who smiled and gave her a wink. They both knew this was the best birthday cake ever.

"Each girl blows out one side of the cake," Mrs. Spitzer explained, putting the cake down on the corner of the table. "Come on over here, birthday girls."

Shirley and Lexie walked up to the cake. For a few

seconds, they looked at each other in the soft light of the burning candles. As she stared at Shirley's smiling face, Lexie felt a glow of pride. She knew she'd played a big part in helping Shirley have a good party this year. Maybe the two of them would do the same thing again next year.

"Happy birthday, Shirley," she said as she got ready to blow out the candles.

"Happy birthday, Lexie."

THIRTEEN

The following Wednesday Lexie came home from school and found her mother lying down on the couch in the living room. Mrs. Nielsen was munching on a handful of peanuts left over from the birthday party and absentmindedly turning the pages of a *Consumer Reports* magazine.

Lexie stood in the doorway and gaped. It occurred to her then that she almost never saw her mother even *sitting* down, not to mention *lying* down. Without taking off the beautiful new shiny satin Minnesota Twins jacket her family had given her for her birthday, Lexie rushed over to her mother's side.

"Mom! What's the matter? Are you sick?"

Mrs. Nielsen shook her head and closed the magazine. "No, I'm just taking a few minutes off," she said. "I'm feeling a little let down, I guess."

Lexie sat down on the edge of the couch. "Because my birthday party's over, you mean?"

"Well, no, actually that's not the reason, believe it or not. It's because Penelope Dove lost the school board election yesterday."

"She did? Gosh, Mom, that's too bad. After all that hard work you did."

Mrs. Nielsen swung her legs around and sat up. "Oh, it's not so bad, honey," she said. "To tell you the truth, none of us ever really believed Penelope had much chance of winning. She's just a bit too . . . offbeat, I guess. You remember what the people we talked to said about her that night. She just seems to impress everybody as being a little strange."

Lexie was confused. "But, Mom, if you *knew* she was probably going to lose, why'd you do all that work for her campaign?"

Her mother shrugged. "There's really no sensible answer to that, Lex, except to say that I felt I had to do it. I believed Penelope was *right*—weird, but right."

She glanced at her watch and got to her feet. "Enough of this wallowing in self-pity," she said. "If I start right now, I can get in an hour's work on my thesis proposal before Karen gets home from chorus practice and wants to use the computer."

Lexie got up and followed her mother into the kitchen. "Say, Mom," she said, "I've got a great idea. You have all the same beliefs as Penelope Dove, but you're not weird, so . . ."

"Why, thank you, Lexie," Mrs. Nielsen interrupted with a laugh. "I'll accept that as a real compliment."

"Let me finish, Mom. You have the same beliefs as Penelope Dove, but you're not weird, so why don't *you* run for a place on the school board?"

Her mother paused and turned around to look at her. "Lexie," she said, "if the family thinks I'm busy now, what do you think they'd say if I were on the school board? Those poor people don't have a minute to call their own!"

"We could handle it, Mom."

"Well, I couldn't! Not at this point, anyway." She walked through the kitchen and opened the door to the basement.

"Let me know if you change your mind," Lexie called after her. "I'll be your campaign manager. We'd be a great team."

Mrs. Nielsen turned away from the door, recrossed the kitchen floor, and gave her daughter a hug.

"Thanks, Lexie," she said. "But I think we already are a great team!"

Lexie smiled and watched her mother walk back over to the basement door and go downstairs. Then she opened the cupboard and started searching for the peanut butter.